S0-BSZ-721

"What's your rush?"

Cole guided Tess toward the car. "We have a lot of talking to do."

She inhaled his scent of sweat, dirt and horse. *This is what home smells like.* This was also what 100 percent man felt like. At that sudden realization, she pulled away from him.

He lifted her chin. "What's the matter, sweetheart?" he challenged. "Have you forgotten what a real man is?"

Tess tried to squirm past Cole, and succeeded only in wedging herself more tightly against him. The length of his body pressed against her made Tess all too aware of the danger that lurked behind his mischievous grin. She'd wind up in a whole mess of trouble if she remained in this position much longer.

Cole ran his hands leisurely down her sides. Shock registered the moment Tess realized what he was about to do.

'Cole...please...don't."

Cole's powerful fingers danced along her sides, tickling her.

"Okay, okay—you win!" she gasped, laughing. "We'll talk, but later, all right?"

Tess looked up at Cole. She couldn't remember when she'd last laughed. How did he always seem to know what she needed most?

Dear Reader,

Horses are one of my greatest passions in life. When I first heard about hippotherapy, I was astounded by the amount of mobility a person could gain by sitting astride this magnificent animal. Different than therapeutic riding, hippotherapy is a form of physical and occupational therapy that utilizes the movement of the horse to treat various conditions from arthritis to traumatic brain injuries. After I discovered how children afflicted with cerebral palsy greatly benefited from this specific type of therapy, *Home to the Cowboy* was born, and so was the sweetest little girl named Ever.

A very special thanks to Heather Hussong at Hope Cottage in Dallas, Texas, for enlightening me about all the beautiful children available for adoption, and to Kaye Marks at PATH International in Denver, Colorado, for opening my eyes to the wondrous benefits of hippotherapy.

To the therapists, foster families and adoptive parents who give so much of themselves to change the lives of our world's children...simply put, you are amazing.

Home to the Cowboy is the sequel to *Betting on Texas*. Come back to Ramblewood and the Langtry family, where there's never a dull moment on the Bridle Dance Ranch. Feel free to stop in and visit me at www.amandarenee.com. I'd love to hear from you. Happy reading!

Amanda Renee

HOME
TO THE
COWBOY

—

AMANDA RENEE

HARLEQUIN® AMERICAN ROMANCE®

If you purchased this book without a cover you should be aware that this book is stolen property. It was reported as "unsold and destroyed" to the publisher, and neither the author nor the publisher has received any payment for this "stripped book."

Recycling programs
for this product may
not exist in your area.

ISBN-13: 978-0-373-75468-7

HOME TO THE COWBOY

Copyright © 2013 by Amanda Renee Mayo

All rights reserved. Except for use in any review, the reproduction or utilization of this work in whole or in part in any form by any electronic, mechanical or other means, now known or hereafter invented, including xerography, photocopying and recording, or in any information storage or retrieval system, is forbidden without the written permission of the publisher, Harlequin Enterprises Limited, 225 Duncan Mill Road, Don Mills, Ontario M3B 3K9, Canada.

This is a work of fiction. Names, characters, places and incidents are either the product of the author's imagination or are used fictitiously, and any resemblance to actual persons, living or dead, business establishments, events or locales is entirely coincidental.

This edition published by arrangement with Harlequin Books S.A.

For questions and comments about the quality of this book, please contact us at CustomerService@Harlequin.com.

® and ™ are trademarks of Harlequin Enterprises Limited or its corporate affiliates. Trademarks indicated with ® are registered in the United States Patent and Trademark Office, the Canadian Trade Marks Office and in other countries.

Printed in U.S.A.

ABOUT THE AUTHOR

Born and raised in the northeast, Amanda Renee currently resides on the Intracoastal Waterway in sunny South Carolina. Her dreams came true when she was discovered through Harlequin's So You Think You Can Write contest.

When not creating stories about love, laughter and things that go bump in the night, she enjoys the company of her schnoodle named Duffy, traveling, photography, playing guitar and anything involving horses. You can visit her at www.amandarenee.com.

Books by Amanda Renee

HARLEQUIN AMERICAN ROMANCE
1442—BETTING ON TEXAS

For Laura Marie Altom, my friend and mentor.

Thank you for being my voice of reason, and for the countless sanity checks.

And to Little Ricky—my faithful companion for thirteen years.

Chapter One

A loud caterwaul rose from the backseat of Tess Dalton's rental car as she crossed over Cooter Creek.

"We're almost there." The tires thumped against the wooden boards of the old steel bridge, increasing her tabby's anxiety. "Oh! What in heaven's name is that smell?"

Ricky's stink bomb was the cherry on her already bountiful sundae. At least she'd had the foresight to pack a disposal kitty-litter box. Tess traveled the country over with her beloved feline and, never fail, he did it every time. She thanked the stars above it hadn't happened on the plane. They probably would've declared an emergency landing due to toxic warfare if it had.

The noxious odors filling her car added one more page to Tess's book of highlights for the week. Her swift, security-assisted escort off the aircraft the moment it touched down deserved its own chapter. Ricky's rendition of "Cat Scratch Fever" wasn't exactly the cabin crew's idea of in-flight entertainment. But did they really have to applaud when she exited the plane?

No matter the hassle, Tess wouldn't have it any other way. Ricky was the one constant in her life, and wherever she went, he went.

The fall foliage lined the narrow two-lane highway in brilliant shades of crimson and gold. The sun peeked over the corrugated roof of Slater's Mill, gilding the honky-tonk's parking lot in a warm glow. It always amazed Tess how beautiful the most mundane things appeared when bathed in the morning light. The luminous orb didn't drop by her New York City apartment until almost noontime.

"Everything's the same." She draped her arms across the top of the steering wheel, peering through the windshield at the old brick-front buildings, decorated for Halloween with bats and scary cats.

Change was inevitable in New York. You went to sleep with a deli on the corner and woke to a dry cleaner in its place. Not in Ramblewood, the land where time stood still.

A horn startled Tess.

"Whoops! Sorry." Tess waved to the man behind her. She drove another block and angled her car in front of the Magpie Luncheonette.

Located in the heart of town, the Magpie began as a bakery. Her mother wanted to call the place Maggie's Buns but Tess's father, Henry, put the kibosh on the idea the moment she uttered the words. Naming it "the Magpie" was his idea. It was appropriate, since her mother and her friends lived to chat and gossip and were downright busybodies. The townsfolk flocked to the Magpie for their coffee and quick meals while they caught up on who was involved with who and what was new in town. Henry never understood why Ramblewood still bothered to print a newspaper. You could get more information in five minutes at the Magpie than if you read the *Gazette* from cover to cover.

There was a chill in the fresh fall, cat-poop-free air.

She grabbed her sweatshirt from the passenger seat and stretched, stepping from the car. Shrugging the buttery-yellow fleece over her head, Tess felt the muscles in her legs throb from the red-eye flight and drive in from the airport.

Removing the offending care package Ricky had thoughtfully left for her, Tess pulled the carrier into the shade of the backseat with one hand, digging into her purse for a bottle of hand sanitizer with the other.

"I'll be right back." She tossed the Baggie into the garbage can near the curb.

Surveying the treats on display in the luncheonette's grand picture window made her feel like a kid again. Every day, on her way home from school, Tess played a guessing game to figure out which treat her mother had baked. Kentucky Sky-High Pie had been her favorite and still was to this day.

Maggie had started the patisserie when Tess was four, hoping to bring a little cultural flair to the town. By Tess's tenth birthday, the bakery had grown into the luncheonette. Maggie's little eatery was a favorite with the locals for a quick bite, but no matter how successful or busy Maggie was, she always found time for her only child.

A familiar cowbell sounded from above the door as heavenly aromas greeted Tess, causing immediate salivation. "One of these days that bell is going to fall off and clunk someone right on the head," she grumbled.

"Isn't that the truth?" A striking redhead stepped out from behind the counter. "Girl, it's been way too long!"

"Bridgett!" Tess hugged her old friend. "You look amazing!"

Bridgett spun around in the middle of the restaurant with the grace of a runway model. She stopped when a bell dinged from behind the counter, letting her know her order was up. "Meet me at Slater's tonight so I can catch up on your exciting life in New York and that cretin you almost married."

Almost married.

Her ex-fiancé, Tim, hadn't really given her much of a choice. While Tess was home selecting flower arrangements with their wedding planner, Tim was in Las Vegas eloping with his assistant. What was it about that city? It wasn't the first time she'd been scorned by someone in Vegas, because despite the tourism commercial, not everything that happened there stayed there. At least Tim had had the courtesy to do it before the wedding and not leave her at the altar. The thought alone made her heart stop beating for a few seconds. *Mortified* would have been the understatement of the year.

"Hey, Bert," Tess called to the chef through the kitchen window. He was her father's best friend and an honorary member of their family. Tess even spent the first few years of her life thinking he was one of her uncles. "Give us a minute out here, will you."

"Well, I'll be!" Bert cried out. "Just arrived in town and already causing trouble by monopolizing my sole waitress today. Your mama's at Bridle Dance if you're looking for her."

"Excuse me, ma'am." A petite teenage girl squeezed past Tess and handed Bridgett the check. The word *ma'am* stung Tess like a hornet on a rampage. She was barely thirty-one, and even though she stood beside Bridgett, who was four years younger, she certainly wasn't a ma'am in her book.

"Your mom and Kay are testing some new pastry recipes for Jesse's wedding," Bridgett said as she collected the girl's money. "Maggie didn't expect you until later today."

"I caught an earlier flight."

Tess dreaded going to the Bridle Dance Ranch. She loved the Langtrys—Kay and her four sons—but she didn't want to run into Cole. Friends since the day they were born, they were practically raised side by side like siblings. Once they'd graduated high school, he'd visited Tess in New York and she'd met up with him on the rodeo circuit. After years of flirtation, they gave in to their feelings and took a chance on romance. That is until the Las Vegas National Finals Rodeo in December two years ago, when the half-naked buckle bunnies that followed him from town to town kept throwing themselves at him—correction, throwing their tops at him. He not only seemed to enjoy it, he appeared to have had intimate knowledge of more than one of his faithful followers.

Yes, her attraction to Cole had been undeniable, but Tess wouldn't lower herself to compete with groupies for his affections. She'd had enough of that in school when every female within a twenty-mile range fought to be on the receiving end of his megawatt smile. A long-distance relationship was an impossible proposition anyway. New York City didn't have much use for cowboys unless they were standing on the street corner with a guitar in their tighty whiteys, and she wouldn't give up the lifestyle she worked so hard to achieve just to traipse through cow pastures in Texas.

"I'll catch up with you both a little later."

Tess plucked a handful of cookies from the pink linen-lined basket on the counter. Walking toward the door, she pulled her shoulders backward until she heard a crack between them. A nice hot bath in her parents' antique claw-foot tub would ease the stiffness of the morning.

Settled in the front seat of her car, Tess looked at her reflection in the rearview mirror. A wild mass of auburn layers framed her face. Her one attempt at a trendy chin-length hairstyle earlier in the year was still in its growing-out phase. Pushing a few strands behind her ears and her face devoid of makeup, she braved another glance and pressed on the bags under her eyes, willing them to go away.

"Heard you were coming to town."

"Cole Langtry!" Tess fumbled for her sunglasses, trying in vain to cover the signs of her fatigue. "You scared me half to death."

"You sure are a sight for sore eyes." Cole tilted back his black Stetson, resting one arm on the open window.

"Aren't you as sweet as a slop jar?" Tess hissed.

"Don't go getting yourself worked into a lather." He gave her a mischievous wink. "Step on out of there and give me a proper hello."

Before Tess could respond, Cole opened her door and took her hand in his, leading her from the sedan.

"Ford Focus, huh? I figured you more the convertible or sports car type." He tapped on the side window. "Hey, Rickster. It's been a long time."

Tess released herself from his grasp. "Listen, I'm really sorry about your dad. How is your mom doing?"

"Better than she was." Cole jammed his hands into the pockets of his jeans. "It was a shock to everyone and you knew my dad—stubborn as all get-out. At the first sign of chest pains he should have gone to the hospital, but he ignored it and thought a good night's sleep would cure everything."

"I should have come sooner." Tess braved meeting his gaze.

"Yep, you should have." Cole pursed his lips, moving away from her. "Everyone thought you'd come to the funeral, especially me. But you're here now, so maybe we can talk about what happened in Vegas."

"What did my mother do, tell the entire town Tim married that floozy?" Tess shook her head in disgust. She prided herself on being a private person, not the subject du jour at the Magpie.

"I meant when you ran out on me two years ago." Cole removed his hat so she clearly saw his face. "Not how your boyfriend cheated on you."

"Fiancé—we were engaged, and I didn't run out on you. I'm surprised you noticed, considering your hands were pretty full."

"Ouch!" Cole placed his hand over his heart in a mock attempt to appear wounded. "If I meant that much, you wouldn't have hightailed it back to the big city at the first sign of a couple of rodeo honeys. Jealousy never did look good on you."

If it were only that simple.

Cole was known for his penchant for the female persuasion, going through women like he changed underwear. *If he wore any.* Despite his string of trophy girls, it hadn't stopped Tess from thinking they'd had a chance at a meaningful and monogamous relationship.

The main reason she'd flown out to Vegas that week was to tell him how much he meant to her. The signs they were moving forward were there, or so she thought. In the end, Tess realized it was more than the buckle bunnies. It was the reality that neither one of them was willing to uproot themselves for the other. His groupies merely opened her eyes a bit wider.

"Let's agree to disagree and leave Vegas in the past."

Cole leaned against his truck and looked at her. "What happened to you?"

"What?" Tess glanced across the street toward the Curl Up and Dye Salon. A facial and a haircut were in order before the day was through. "I'm fine, Cole."

"I fully expected ten minutes of banter, five at the very least. Did New York suck out your soul? The Tess I knew wouldn't give up so easily."

"I'm sure I don't understand what you mean." She didn't have to look up at him to know he was still scrutinizing her.

"Since we're getting things out in the open, yes I heard about your *ex-fiancé,* and if you don't mind me saying, you're better off without him."

"I do mind because it's none of your business, or anyone else's for that matter."

"Come on, Tess, this is Ramblewood. Everyone's in everybody else's business."

So much for reassurance that she'd survive the next few weeks with her dignity intact. Small-town gossip was something she'd learned to live without when she moved to New York. In a city that big, it was easy to become another face in the crowd. Everyone was so wrapped up in their own lives they didn't care what was going on in yours.

"I miss New York already." Tess slid into the ice-blue rental and started the engine. "Again, Cole, I'm really sorry. Your dad was an incredible man. I'm sure I'll see you around."

"I guarantee it." Cole stood firm at the window. "But I hope, when I do, you'll have found some of that old feistiness we love."

Tess saw an impish glint in his bourbon-colored eyes

before he stepped aside. It wouldn't take much persuading to get caught up in them for a lifetime. *Had he always looked this good?*

"I, uh—I need to get going." Shaking her head of the salacious thoughts that churned in her mind, she scrambled for an escape. "It was a long flight and I'm anxious to unwind a bit."

"Your mom's out at my place." Cole slapped his hand down on the hood of the Ford. "You know you're always welcome there and we have a few things to catch up on."

He tipped his hat, nodded and turned to walk into the Magpie. Tess peered over the top of her Ray-Bans. No man could possibly compete with the way Cole's jeans fit across his backside.

With the center of town and Cole behind her, Tess pulled into her parents' gravel driveway. A wisteria-covered arbor stood at the entrance of the slate walk leading to the two-story cream-colored farmhouse. The purple blooms were breathtaking in the spring, but this time of year, the vines had a more mysterious charm, which her mother enhanced with artificial Halloween cobwebs and festive scarecrows.

Spanish moss danced in the breeze as it swung from the gnarled boughs of the majestic live oak in the front yard. Throughout the sweltering Texas summers, the tree shaded the impeccable front yard. Tess never figured out how her mother found the energy to run the luncheonette and still accomplish the countless gardening projects she did every year.

Ricky caterwauled once again.

"Okay, little guy." She hauled the carrier out of the car along with the rest of her luggage. "Let's get you inside."

Tess climbed the pumpkin-lined porch stairs, reaching into her handbag for the key she'd carried since the day she left for college. She knew she should have taken it off her key ring years ago, but there was comfort in realizing she could always go home again. Stopping short of trying the lock, Tess turned the knob and the door opened.

Four dead bolts on Tess's New York apartment door gave her a sense of security. Her parents, on the other hand, had never locked a door in their lives.

The spacious living room and kitchen combination always reminded Tess of *The Waltons*. The stairs to the left displayed old-fashioned milk bottles on each step. When dairies began to phase out glass bottles in favor of wax cartons and plastic jugs, Maggie had started saving every one she found.

Tess ascended the old staircase, relishing the familiar squeaks and groans of the wood. Stark white linen walls replaced the tiny pale wild-rose print wallpaper in her former bedroom. A lone oil painting of yellow roses hung on the wall opposite the door. A rough, unstained pine bed now stood where her four-poster once had. Her mother had changed the room shortly after she went to college, but Tess still missed the one place of comfort she'd always retreated to when she was younger. That room was probably the only thing that had changed in this town during the past thirteen years.

She opened the wire door of the carrier. Ricky hesitated and then strolled out, arching his back and stretching his legs one by one.

"I know how you feel, little man." The cat looked up at Tess and let out a soft meow. He padded over, rubbed alongside her leg and purred loudly. "I hear your motor running."

She picked up her favorite male companion and gave

him a gentle squeeze before setting him on the bed. Leaning beside the window, Tess looked out across the yard, which was enclosed by a picket fence. As if it were yesterday, she remembered her father pushing her on the old tire swing that still hung from the hickory tree.

The frenzied way her mother chased her prized Silkie chickens around the coop provided comic relief for the neighbors within earshot. The coop remained, but the chickens were long gone.

Tess inhaled sharply when the image of Tim's face interrupted her trip down memory lane. She'd come here to forget the two-timing rat of a man. Sorting through the entire secretary elopement situation wasn't easy. Tim had his flaws like everyone else, but running off to marry Rachel was the last thing she'd expected. Hell, the woman was in the wedding party, at Tim's insistence, of course. Why hadn't she seen the signs sooner?

Tim's deceit had sent Tess into a tailspin. Why had she wasted almost two years on that poor excuse of a human being? She'd cried all night on her roommate Cheryl-Leigh's shoulder. And when she'd thought things couldn't get any worse, she had gone to work the next day and found out the recent corporate merger had left her jobless.

Executive management told her they were "trimming the fat." She must have been a little chubby, because she was one of the first to go. Cheryl-Leigh remained employed at the web design company where they'd both worked, and Tess harbored a little resentment toward her best friend because of it. They were supposed to be a team.

Jesse Langtry's wedding had come at just the right time. It was the break she needed to put some distance between her and the pain. Unable to take a real vacation over the past few years, Tess welcomed the chance to come home for more than a long weekend. Although she wasn't quite sure what to do with herself during the day, since everyone she knew in town had a job.

Her phone vibrated in her pocket. Another text message from one of her friends asking if she'd found Mr. Right at the airport. Clichéd as it sounded, she'd met Tim in an airport bar and her friends had yet to let her live it down.

Tess headed downstairs and crossed the wide-planked hardwood floor. She remembered her grandfather's weekend visits to help lay the flooring and lend an extra hand with the renovations. She had been barely five when her parents bought the old house, but she recalled how much work it had needed when they first moved in. She loved New York, but there was something about the familiarity of home that tugged at her heart.

Her grade school photos were arranged on the table next to the couch. Riding trophies lined the top of the fireplace mantel. Trophies she had won thanks to Cole's father, Joe, and his countless hours of lessons. And how did she thank the man? She missed his funeral.

In the kitchen, Tess ran her hand down the front of the refrigerator over the magnets she'd sent home from her travels abroad. Anyone entering the house felt the love the Daltons had for their daughter and one another. Sometimes Tess felt guilty for not visiting more often.

It was still a few hours before her father came home for lunch. Pouring herself a glass of sweet tea, Tess sat on the front porch swing. She rocked back and forth, the worn cedar boards creaking beneath her. Ricky jumped up and lay down beside her, his tail swishing, enjoying the freedom from his earlier confinement.

"I had my first kiss on this swing." Tess scratched the cat behind his ears while he purred contently. "Cole Langtry." She whispered his name for fear if she said it aloud he would suddenly appear.

They were in the sixth grade and inseparable. One afternoon, when they were swinging, he'd grabbed and kissed her. Tess was so angry she hauled off and punched him. It was their first and last kiss until they were adults. They were close throughout junior and senior high school and even attended prom together when Travis Gardner stood Tess up at the last minute so he could compete in a rodeo. Scheduled for the same event, Cole chose to escort Tess instead, telling her he would do anything to stop her tears. They were crowned king and queen of the prom, and even though the night was magical, he didn't try to kiss her again and they didn't pursue anything more than friendship until a few years ago.

Tess stared at the empty glass she held. She didn't remember drinking a single sip of the cool liquid. She jumped off the swing, causing it to bang the porch railing and launch her cat through the air. "Whoops! At least you landed on your feet."

She scooped the angry tabby up in one arm and stormed into the house. Why couldn't she get that blasted man out of her head? The screen door slammed behind her. One day her father would finally fix that broken spring. She picked up the phone to call the ranch and then hesitated, placing it on the kitchen counter.

Outside, Tess unloaded the rest of her belongings from the trunk of the rental and began carrying them into the house while she debated what to do next. Take a nice hot bath or unpack? The heels of her boots dug deep into the ground.

Come on, eat your crow and get it over with. Tess knew she owed Kay Langtry a personal apology for missing her husband's funeral. Repeated excuses via her mother only went so far and the woman deserved more respect than that. Guilt weighed heavily on Tess's mind and the sooner she made amends, the sooner her conscience would stop haunting her.

Gravel flew as she jammed the key into the ignition and stepped on the gas. Without warning, the car jolted when the rear tire drove over something hard.

"What the—" Tess opened the door to see half of her luggage wedged under the car. Preoccupied with thoughts of the Langtrys, she'd forgotten about the rest of her bags. She grabbed the suitcase handle and yanked hard. It broke off in her hand, hurling her backward onto the ground. Tess sat in disbelief, staring at her expensive designer luggage.

"The perfect way to end a perfect week!" Losing all self-control, she started to laugh and felt the stress begin to leave her body. It was either laugh or cry, and at this very moment, laughter did truly feel like the best medicine.

"Are you all right, dear?" Her parent's neighbor, Janie Anderson, stood at the end of the driveway, her Yorkie pulling toward Tess on a retractable leash. The giant pink polka-dotted bow on the top of the dog's head seemed to make the situation even more humorous.

"Hey, Mrs. Anderson! Good to see you again!" Tess waved hello, then collapsed into another fit of laughter. Janie shook her head and continued with her walk. Still lying in the driveway, she propped herself up on her elbows and looked at the suitcases. "Let's try this again."

Tess stood, dusting off her jeans, and proceeded to

struggle, kick and swear until she managed to free her suitcases and set them in the house. Then she took a deep breath and headed out to the Langtry ranch to apologize.

COLE HAD KNOWN for a few weeks that Tess was flying into town today and had been psyching himself up to meet her fiancé. When Maggie informed him the wedding was off, he'd chastised himself for the slight elation he'd felt at the news Tess was single again.

No, he'd rather drive his pickup over one of his championship belt buckles than give that woman an ounce of his heart again.

Tess had always seen him as a trusting, reliable friend, but the feelings Cole had had for her in high school grew stronger each time they visited one another after graduation. Tired of wondering what might be, two years ago Cole grabbed the bull by the horns and told Tess how he really felt. He'd been relieved to hear she had the same feelings for him, but annoyed he'd wasted so much energy on women who had meant nothing to him. The two of them made things official and started dating, but the long distance was difficult.

Although they made the relationship work with frequent trips, it grew harder to say goodbye and Cole was set to show Tess how much she meant to him by proposing. Always one to take a ride on the wild side, he knew how much she loved spontaneity and adventure. The night was meticulously arranged with his brother Shane's assistance. A private roller-coaster ride high above the Stratosphere, followed by a four-course chef's tasting menu at the Top of the World restaurant, would lead to a proposal as they overlooked one of the world's most exciting cities.

For the second half of Tess's surprise, Cole pre-booked the Stratosphere wedding chapel for Valentine's Day in hopes she'd love the idea of a destination wedding. But the chance to slip a ring on her finger never came.

When he and Tess walked out of the Thomas & Mack Center that evening after his victorious ride, he was blindsided by a couple of topless groupies. That in it-self wouldn't have been so bad, but when one of the women asked when they were going to spend another night together, Tess flew out of the parking lot before he had an opportunity to explain. The truth was he *had* been with each of them before, on more than one occasion but never at the same time, and he couldn't blame Tess for assuming the worst of him. Before he was able to tell her he'd slept with them *before* he and Tess started dating, Tess had checked out of the hotel. He knew his ladies' man reputation was bad, but after their past few months together, he'd thought she under-stood where his heart was, even though he hadn't actu-ally said the words.

Hopping mad, Cole took his anger out on the rodeo and overrode every event, making one careless mis-take after another and destroying any chance he had of winning. He still blamed Tess for that loss, although she wouldn't know it, considering he hadn't heard from her again with the exception of a brief voice mail when his father died. When she didn't show up for the fu-neral, he didn't bother to return her call. Now she was in town for his brother Jesse's wedding and there was no avoiding her, especially since both of their mothers were handling the reception.

The Bridle Dance Ranch, one of the state's largest paint and quarter cutting horse ranches, left Cole with little time on his hands. The newly added sod farm division was still in its infancy and had probably been one of his father's better concepts, but Cole and his brothers' lack of knowledge in the field added to Cole's daily stress. Refusing to give Tess a second thought, he had successfully blocked her out of his mind until his father's death. Although he'd been surrounded by friends and family, she was the one person he wanted around, and she had kept her distance.

"I heard Tess is in town." Jesse sat on the stool beside Cole at the Magpie counter. "How are you holding up?"

"How the hell did you hear that? I just saw her a few minutes ago myself."

"Ferris was behind her and said she was parked in the middle of the street, looking around. Had to toot the horn to get her to move."

"It's been two years," Cole growled. "Maybe she forgot what the place looked like."

"Still a sore subject, even after seeing her, huh?" Jesse asked.

"I told her we need to talk, but who knows? I used to be able to predict how she'd react to any given situation, but not anymore. She seems different."

"She got dumped and lost her job," Jesse stated. "What do you expect?"

"It's more than that." Cole stood, placing his hat on his head. "The fire that always got her in so much trouble is gone."

"She'll come around." Jesse motioned for his usual breakfast order. "Call me later so we can go over the plans for the ranch."

Cole slapped his brother on the shoulder and headed out the door. He knew Jesse still carried guilt from not resolving the decade-and-a-half-long falling-out he'd had with their father. When the will was read, everyone was surprised to hear Jesse's name included with his brothers as one of the ranch's stockholders. Although Jesse in no way wanted anything to do with Bridle Dance, his father had respected him for working to create a legacy of his own training horses at the Double Trouble Ranch without any of the family's financial resources.

Nonetheless, Bridle Dance was Jesse's birthright and he wanted to memorialize their father, with Cole and their mother's help, by fulfilling Joe's dream of converting part of Bridle Dance into a hippotherapy center. Joe had visited a similar facility and had seen how a horse's movements were used to treat people with injuries and physical disabilities. Cole was overjoyed when Jesse voted for opening their own facility *and* pledged his share of the profits from the rest of the ranch to the project.

Due to the size of the Langtrys' business, Joe had the foresight to name Cole's mother, Kay, and attorney Henry Dalton, Tess's father, as coexecutors of the estate. Joe's will bequeathed the house, the land and their small winery to Kay, and the business side of the ranch was to be split evenly between the four brothers. The land itself was leased back to the Bridle Dance Ranch Corporation, providing Kay with a lifetime income.

The corporate bylaws stated every major financial decision involving the ranch required a majority vote, and without a say in the business, Kay was at the mercy of her children where Dance of Hope, the hippotherapy facility, was concerned. And since each sibling held a twenty-five-percent stake in the company, the brothers were at a standoff.

Cole and Jesse were determined to honor their father

and bring the nonprofit to fruition, but Shane and Chase didn't share that vision. They went along with it when Joe was alive because they didn't have any other choice. They wanted to build an over-the-top, world-class rodeo school instead.

Cole had to find a way to change his brothers' minds and he'd stop at nothing to see the project through. He needed to focus his attention on the ranch, not Tess, yet somehow, she kept popping into his head. Memories of her scent, the touch of her hand in his, even her tousled hair were singeing the outer shell of his heart.

But that book was closed and he refused to reopen it.

Chapter Two

The words *Bridle Dance* balanced between two rearing bronze horses located on either side of the dirt road. Despite the Langtrys' wealth, Tess loved that they'd never paved the entrance, preserving the ranch's historic appeal. Rows of pecan trees heavy with fruit formed thick canopies above her. She hoped they'd be harvested while she was in town.

Through the fretwork of tree branches, she could see the sprawling three-story main house. If there was such a thing as a log manor, this was it. A porch produced from the same golden timbers spanned the front of the home, welcoming family and friends to relax and enjoy the sprawling landscape.

She caught a glimpse of Cole in the distance, mounted on a sleek black horse. He removed his Stetson and ran his hand through his thick brown hair before turning to eye her warily.

Gripping the steering wheel, she revved the car hard. With a wave of his hat, Cole signaled his horse into a full gallop. Tess floored the gas pedal, her tires spinning. Clouds of dirt encircled the car before it shot forward.

Machine versus beast took them back in time to

when they were teenagers. Tess would try to best one of Cole's prized quarter horses with a ranch rig. The horse always won.

History repeated, Cole reined his mount beside the front porch. Tess jerked the wheel to the left, braked hard and fishtailed to a stop on the other side.

Cole nudged his gelding to the driver's side door. Before Tess placed one booted foot out of the vehicle, he was off his mount and blocking her path.

"Pretty impressive for a rental, but I win again." He placed both hands on the door frame to prevent her escape, motioning with his head to the horse behind him. "But Blackjack here is the real winner. Although I'm afraid I might have to spend the next month unlearning this *race toward home* trick we just taught him. Remember how Captain Chaos threw riders when he charged the stables after he came off the trails?"

"Do I ever." Tess ducked under his arms. "Your dad was furious with us for racing."

Cole grabbed her by the waist before she had a chance to flee.

"What's your rush?" He guided her back toward the car. "We have a lot of talking to do."

She inhaled the scent of sweat, dirt and horse. Home. *This is what home smells like*. This was also what one hundred percent man felt like. At that sudden realization, she pulled away from him.

A rough, callused hand lifted her chin. "What's the matter, sweetheart?" he challenged. "Have you forgotten what a real man is?"

Tess tried to squirm past Cole but only succeeded in wedging herself tighter between car and cowboy. The length of him pressed against her made Tess all too aware of the danger that lurked behind his mischievous grin. She'd wind up in a whole mess of trouble if she remained in this position much longer.

"Is my mother here?" Struggling to avoid his eyes, she stared instead at his chest. The corded muscles were unmistakably visible through his taut fawn-colored thermal shirt. She felt the urge to run her hands underneath it and trace each ripple with her fingers.

"In the house, but I didn't tell her you were here. Figured you'd like to do the honors."

He ran his hands leisurely down her sides and tightly gripped her waist.

Shock registered the moment Tess realized what he was about to do.

"Cole, please don't." She grabbed at his hands, trying in vain to pry them away. "Not that!"

Cole's powerful fingers dug into her sides, tickling her. She twisted in his arms, her knees buckling.

"Okay, okay—you win!" she said in between shallow breaths. "We'll talk, but later, all right? Let me go see my mom."

Tess looked up at Cole. She couldn't remember the last time she'd laughed. When had life become so serious and complicated?

The noonday sun upon his face contrasted the shadow of the previous night's beard. Tess reached out to stroke his cheek but withdrew before making contact. She refused to fall into that trap again. She hated to admit it, but being here with him felt good, although she knew Cole probably would never forgive her for missing his dad's funeral. The most she could hope for was to put the past to rest and start over again.

Would Kay Langtry accept her apology? Tess didn't know where to begin without sounding selfish. The problem was her reasons *were* selfish. She'd wanted to avoid Cole, even though she had seriously considered flying home. She'd also wanted to avoid a major blowup with Tim. He didn't want her going back home without him and he wouldn't miss work to attend the funeral of someone he'd never met. Tim wasn't interested in seeing where she came from, no matter how hard Tess tried to convince him. How could she love a man like that? The signs were there, but she'd been oblivious to them day after day.

"It'll work itself out." Years might have passed, but Cole could still read her emotions.

"I hate it when you do that. I was never able to put anything past you." Tess faced her old friend. "I truly am sorry."

Cole turned her toward the porch stairs, placing his hands on her shoulders, and gave her a push.

"It's not me you have to apologize to."

Tess sighed and hesitantly clambered up the porch stairs and entered the house. Rustic log walls reached up toward a bevy of skylights in the Langtrys' great room. Hand-hewn wood beams led to a large open loft. Intricate beaded artwork from the Native American Kickapoo tribe decorated the far wall leading to the kitchen. Plush, cognac leather sofas formed a horseshoe before a monumental, floor-to-ceiling river-rock fireplace.

The house was indulgent, yet it swathed you in warmth and comfort the moment you stepped within its depths. Tess headed for the dining room, stopping when she overheard her mother and Kay's voices.

"I'm so glad Tess is still coming to the wedding," Kay, her mother's best friend, said from beyond the kitchen wall. "It hurts me to think of her staying in New York by herself."

"It hasn't been easy for her" came Maggie's reply.

"She still has her roommate, but I think that relationship's a little strained since Tess was laid off."

"This vacation will do her some good," Kay said. "Maybe she'll move home. You can set those in the other room to cool. I'm afraid we've run out of counter space in here."

Maggie placed a tray of honey-drizzled croissants on the dining table a few yards away from Tess, who flattened herself against a large sideboard, almost gouging her ribs on a deer antler lamp in the process. Her mother would tan her hide if she caught her eavesdropping. A ravenous belly grumble almost betrayed her location. Maggie turned and walked into the kitchen as Tess let out a sigh of relief.

"Shh," Tess whispered. She placed a hand to her abdomen and tried to concentrate on the conversation, not the sweet aroma that beckoned her.

She nearly jumped out of her skin when the screen door creaked behind her. Cole stood in the doorway, the light behind him shadowing his face.

"Lose your way?" Cole placed his hat on the hat rack beside the door.

Tess crept closer to the kitchen to hear more, motioning to him to keep quiet.

"Tess, it's so wonderful to see you!" Cole bellowed. A wide grin spread across his face when he sauntered into the room and grabbed a croissant from the table. Admiring the flaky crust, he broke off a piece and motioned for her to taste it. "These are amazing. Try this before it cools off much more."

Tess shot him a look that would have killed most men on the spot. How dare he give her away! Even worse, he was distracting her with food. Unable to resist a moment longer, she reached for one of her own.

"Here." Cole offered her the other half.

Tess opened her mouth and took the piece from him, almost nipping his fingers.

"Holy hot!" She danced around the dining room, Cole chortling at her pain. "You set me up, you idiot!"

"I thought you were going to take it from me." Cole laughed. "Not bite it right out of my hand."

Maggie and Kay emerged from the kitchen in time to see Tess fanning her face. Caught with her hand in the proverbial cookie jar, Tess fumbled for an excuse to explain her silent entrance into the house.

"Look who's calling who an idiot." Cole jumped up and down flailing his arms, mocking Tess.

"Colburn Joseph Langtry!" Kay threatened. "Put a cork in your pistol."

"Oh—" Tess giggled. "You're in trouble."

"Tessa May Dalton," Maggie howled. "How old are you? Two?"

"Ha-ha!" Cole shouted.

Kay snapped a towel at him, hitting his elbow with a resounding thwack. He held his arm like a wounded child while Tess did her best not to burst out laughing. Nope, life in Ramblewood hadn't changed. At least Cole's antics eased the tension in a potentially strained greeting.

Maggie rushed over and gave her daughter a body-engulfing hug, then held Tess at arm's length to get a better look. Pleased, she drew her in for another clinch.

"We weren't expecting you until tonight," Maggie squealed. "You should have called."

"I took the chance of waiting on standby and got an earlier flight," Tess said. "I hate flying later in the day. It's a waste of valuable hours."

She turned to Cole's mother, who was standing next to her son. "Hello, Kay. How are you?"

Maggie released her daughter as Kay enveloped Tess in a warm embrace.

"Were your ears burning?" Kay asked. "We were talking about you this very minute. My, it sure has been a long time."

Tess knew a subtle reprimand when she heard one. "I'm so sorry for your loss and I sincerely apologize for not being here."

"I'm sure you had your reasons, dear." Kay was polite, but the underlying criticism was clear. "When you're settled, I need your expertise."

"Mom," Cole warned. "What are you up to?"

"Go make yourself useful and check the humidistat in the wine cellar," Kay said. "It felt too damp down there this morning."

Cole's booted feet stomped loudly out of the room. *What was his issue?* Tess wondered. Maggie wet her fingertip and tried to smooth Tess's hair from her face.

"Eww, Mom, stop! I'm aware it looks bad." Before the day was through, Tess needed to do something with her hair. Once her mom started in with the spit styling, she knew she was long overdue for a trim.

"It's nice to see you and Cole made some progress with this mysterious rift between you two," Kay said, once Cole was out of earshot.

"Rift? There's no rift." Tess wasn't surprised to hear Kay didn't know why she and Cole were no longer together. How did a son explain to his mother that his libido had ruined a relationship? "What do you need my expertise on?"

"I don't even know where to begin when it comes to marketing a hippotherapy facility. Since you're here, I'd like to hire you to get us headed in the right direction and really showcase Dance of Hope."

"But I thought that was on hold. Mom told me Shane and Chase are blocking the project from going further."

"Eh!" Kay dismissed the thought. "They'll come to their senses soon enough. I don't want to waste any more time."

"I'm not sure I can help." Working so close to Cole would completely negate the peace and relaxation she'd anticipated for this trip. "I'll be here for a few short weeks, and then I'm heading home."

"Tess, outside." Annoyance registered on Maggie's face.

"Uh, okay, I—"

"Tessa May!"

Use of her full name twice in one day meant her mom was serious even though Tess wasn't sure what she'd done wrong.

"Kay is offering you a paying job and you're second-guessing her?" Maggie chastised her daughter on the porch. "After the crap you pulled this summer, you owe this to her."

"What?" Tess didn't believe her ears. "I have other things going on, Mom."

"And what are they, Miss Big Shot? You don't even have a job."

Tess spun around, "Yes, and thanks for bringing that to all of Ramblewood's attention. I also hear everyone knows Tim ditched me."

"Oh, dear." Maggie furrowed her brow. "I told people the truth. What's the big deal?"

"Mom, it's none of their business." Tess wouldn't allow her mother to twist the situation. Truth or not, no one needed the details of what was going on in her life.

"Second, I can get a job in New York in a heartbeat. What's the harm in my taking a little break to regroup?"

Maggie reached for her daughter's hand and held it in her own. Tess noticed the deep laugh lines in her mother's face, but there was no laughter there now. She watched her mother anxiously push a strand of chestnut hair out of her eyes as she attempted a smile, looking thinner than she had in recent memory.

"Kay is putting aside whatever this…this thing is between you and Cole and offering you an olive branch for not making it to Joe's funeral. The least you can do is take it. You've put a major strain on your father and my relationship with the Langtrys and you need to set things right."

If anyone knew how to shame Tess into doing something, it was Maggie. Tess couldn't blame her mother for being upset when Tess hadn't exactly been the greatest friend to the family that had treated her like one of their own all her life.

"You did what?" Cole was blown away by his mother's revelation after Tess and Maggie left. "How could you hire Tess without consulting with me?"

"Now you know how it feels." Shane stormed through the kitchen door. "You're such a pro at doing things yourself, I guess you came by it honestly."

"Shane, don't—"

"Don't what, Cole?" Shane shrugged. "Stand up for my share in Bridle Dance?"

"Stand up all you want but don't talk about Mom like that." Cole sat at the table next to Kay. "Why did you bring Tess into this?"

"We need her." Kay folded her hands around Cole's. "Look at the corporate websites she's created. She's good at what she does and she knows this family. No one can put the personal touches on our marketing campaign like she can."

"Chase and I won't agree to this." Shane strode across the room. "You're setting yourself up for a big disappointment and then everyone will blame me. Why are you doing this, Mom?"

"Because I'm hoping, by the grace of God, you boys will honor your father's wishes. This was his dream."

"A waste of a dream if you ask me." Shane removed a white porcelain mug off the shagbark hickory cup holder he'd made in Cub Scouts. "Of course, no one gives a hoot what I think."

"Knock it off, Shane," Cole said. "Mom's been through enough and she doesn't need any more."

Shane slammed the mug on the counter with such force, Cole was amazed it didn't shatter.

"We've all been through a lot!" Shane was dangerously close to the table. Cole rose to confront him, a breath separating the two men. "I find it laughable that you and our hypocritical, wayward brother, who never cared one iota about this place, are trying to take control. It's throwing good money after bad and I'll block you at every turn. I've already informed Henry about your continued plans, and as coexecutor of the estate, he'll make sure the corporate bylaws are enforced."

"You called Tess's father?" Kay pushed her way between her sons. "There was no reason to put him in the middle of this, Shane. This is a family dispute and I don't appreciate you involving him."

"He has every right to be involved, Mom. Dad made both of you coexecutors so Henry could handle the business side of Bridle Dance and you wouldn't have to. All I'm doing is keeping him in the loop so he can legally watch out for the ranch's best interest." Shane's expression turned smug. "This is what happens when you continue to move forward with these plans without a majority vote."

"I really wish the two of you would keep the Daltons away from here." Cole threw his arms up in defeat.

"Listen, I have no idea what's been going on with you and Tess, but the Daltons are always welcome in this house," Kay said. "And whether either of you approves of my hiring Tess, you'll just have to deal with it, because she'll be working here with me. You boys may own the ranch, but I own this house and the land, and you'd be wise not to forget it. The Lord's not the only one who can giveth and taketh away around here."

Cole shook his head. "Mom, I don't mean to imply they aren't welcome. But I don't think they need to be involved in this—this battle."

Kay left the room, dismissing her sons with a wave of her hand.

Shane snickered. "Under normal circumstances, I'd pity you for having to tolerate being in the same town as Tess after that stunt in Vegas. But, considering you, Mom and Jesse are trying to force my hand with the ranch, I'm okay with Mom forcing yours with Tess. Payback's a bitch."

Cole had had more than enough of the constant bickering over the ranch's future. It had started the day they elected officers based solely on age and Cole, being the eldest, assumed the role of president. Trying to convince Shane it was nothing more than a title was next to impossible and the power struggle began from that moment forward.

Neither Shane nor Chase appreciated the fact that when Cole retired from the rodeo to take the reins of the expansive ranch, he'd allowed them the extra time to remain active on the circuit.

Cole did have to agree with Shane, however, about their mother hiring Tess without consulting them, even if Tess was the best person for the job. Hopefully she would work remotely, because her close proximity might push him over the edge in more than one way. Just knowing she was back in town was occupying more of his thoughts than he'd believed possible. The woman might be a blessing to his mother, but she was a curse to him.

Chapter Three

The following morning Cole parked his truck in front of the Daltons' house, debating whether to go inside. Why was he so nervous? He felt like a teenager on his first date. An unannounced visit first thing in the morning might not sit well with them, especially since his mom and Shane had thrust Tess and Henry on opposite ends of the Langtry spectrum. That could easily pit father against daughter if Henry blocked Kay from continuing with the hippotherapy facility and pushed Tess out of another job.

What am I doing? Cole didn't care if Tess was employed or not and he certainly wasn't about to let Shane or Chase kill this project. He simply didn't want outsiders involved in their personal dispute.

Cole laughed to himself. This had gone way past a dispute. It had become an all-out family feud and now the Daltons were smack-dab in the middle of it.

Henry Dalton was the Langtry family's attorney, although Joe had kept a bevy of legal representatives for a myriad of reasons. The most recent addition was Cole's old classmate, Jonathan Reese.

Jon had become an unfortunate victim of Joe's machinations when he inadvertently came between Cole's brother Jesse and their father before they had a chance to make peace. Good ol' dad was well-intentioned when he set Jon in motion to block Jesse from buying Double Trouble after the owners died. His plan was meant to force Jesse home to Bridle Dance.

Joe didn't count on his son taking off in the other direction and accepting a cutting horse trainer position in Abilene. Fortunately, that plan changed when he fell in love with Miranda, Double Trouble's new owner. And even though Jesse was only a few miles away, Joe wanted his boys home, on family land. But that was their father—a man who stopped at nothing to keep his family together. Ironically, his death had now torn the family in half.

Cole hated the situation his brothers had forced him into, but at the time he'd figured if they wanted to play, he'd toss his Stetson in the ring. He'd immediately retained Jon as his attorney. Since he moved back to town, Jon was a worthy adversary for Henry Dalton, thanks to his involvement in Joe's constant scheming to keep Jesse on Langtry land and the resulting intimate knowledge he'd gained of Joe's future plans for the ranch. Through the Daltons' leaded-glass door, Cole saw Tess and her father eating breakfast at the kitchen table. Maggie's car wasn't in the driveway, which he assumed meant she was already at the luncheonette. After a slight hesitation, he rapped on the mahogany frame, not wanting to presumptuously walk in.

"Cole." Henry wiped his mouth with a napkin. "Since when do you knock around here? Come on in, sit and have something to eat. Tess rustled up a mess of food."

"Morning, Henry," Cole said. "I didn't want to barge in not knowing where things stood with us, especially since my brother has you fighting his battles against me."

"Nonsense, business is business and this is breakfast. No shoptalk here."

"You heard my dad," Tess said. "Sit."

Tess laid an extra place setting before him and filled a mug with fresh coffee. Her hair was slightly shorter and more tamed than it was yesterday. The length suited her, even though he was used to the long waves she'd had since grade school. The auburn locks graced the nape of her neck, leaving the delicate skin exposed above the edge of her heather-gray sweater.

Shift focus, Cole. She's the enemy. The enemy in matters of the heart, that is. Even though he hated the thought of his mother hiring Tess, she might prove to be one of his strongest allies. She was a webmistress genius and a master at convincing people to see things her way through her designs. He needed her on his side, no matter how much of his own peace of mind he had to sacrifice.

"Thank you." Cole helped himself to a spoonful of scrambled eggs, pancakes and some odd-looking baconlike strips. "Everything looks great."

"It's low-sodium turkey bacon." Henry leaned over and whispered to Cole, "Maggie has me on a restricted diet since—well, since the summer."

"It's all right, Henry." Cole understood his meaning. "Since my father died my mom blames herself every day, wondering if her cooking contributed to his heart attack."

Tess stood beside the table, listening intently while Ricky walked between her ankles in a figure-eight pattern. "I'm sorry, Cole."

"Stop apologizing." Cole placed his hand over hers, immediately wishing he hadn't when he felt the silkiness of her skin. "We've asked ourselves the same question. Jesse blames himself for the stress he caused Dad over the years. I wonder if I'd been around more, maybe he would've had less of a workload. Then I tell myself Dad had enough money to hire more help if things became too much for him to handle. It's speculation and we'll never know. We just have to move on from it."

Guilt was a hard pill to swallow. Cole talked until he was blue in the face, trying to reassure everyone in his family that his father's death wasn't their fault. He wasn't so sure he believed it himself. Many things should have been handled differently, but regardless of how he felt, he was damn certain he'd finish what his father started. He owed the man that much.

"What brings you by?" Henry asked, breaking the heavy silence.

"I'm afraid you'll consider it shoptalk." Cole nervously laughed and leaned down to rub Ricky between the ears.

"Ah." Henry rose from the table. "In that case, I will leave you two alone. I'll be late to the office if I don't get a move on. Thank you for a wonderful breakfast, sweetheart. It's good to have you home."

Henry kissed his daughter on the cheek and shook Cole's hand before he left.

"Refill?" Tess asked, the coffeepot hovering above his mug.

"Yes, please."

"What did you want to talk to me about, or shouldn't I ask?"

Cole sensed Tess's trepidation. They needed to settle what happened in Las Vegas, but she clearly wasn't ready to get into it yet. Not wanting to drive her away when he desperately needed her help, Cole pushed the subject to the backburner.

"There's someplace I'd like to show you." Cole rested his fork on the edge of the plate. "And someone I'd like you to meet."

"This isn't a trap or anything, is it?"

"What?" Cole feigned offense. "I wouldn't think of leading you astray."

"Hmm," Tess said. Ricky jumped into her lap, giving him a questioning look himself. "And the croissant incident was one hundred percent innocent, I presume."

"I plead the Fifth." Cole munched on another piece of turkey bacon. "This stuff isn't half-bad. I could get used to it."

"Oh, you must really want something from me if you're complimenting fake bacon." Tess shook her head. "Where are we going?"

"Someplace you won't soon forget."

THE DRIVE WAS pleasant enough and Tess was thankful she'd brought along her camera. Between the radio and the autumn landscape, she managed to sing, talk and photograph her way around the topic she knew Cole wanted to discuss. She figured he wanted to show her the hippotherapy facility Joe had patterned his plans after. And on the way there, in a vehicle moving at seventy miles an hour, she could no longer avoid the issue looming over them.

She would have succeeded in doing just that if the DJ hadn't started blathering on about the local rodeo champions heading to the National Finals Rodeo in Las Vegas next month. Instantly transported to the scene of the crime, Cole gave her no alternative.

"I never meant to hurt you," Cole said. "But I swear to you, I didn't cheat on you."

"It's in the past." Tess clenched her teeth. "Please leave it there."

"I didn't have the chance to say my piece then and I think you owe me at least that much." Cole continued without waiting for her response. "I walked out of that arena with *you* on my arm. It was plain as day for everyone to see *I was with you.* I know it looked bad when those women showed up, and yes, I had been with them in the past, but I thought you knew me better than that. I may be many things, but a cheater isn't one of them. Our relationship was turning serious and I think you were looking for a way out. When one appeared, you ran with it."

Tess bit back the words she almost uttered. What he said was half-true. She knew the kind of man she *thought* Cole was. It was the stupid grin on his face that night that told her this type of thing had happened before, and he'd enjoyed it when it did. She heard the rodeo cowboy stories and knew a man could only take so much teasing before he gave in to temptation. The absurdity of the situation was that she'd immediately started dating Tim and he wound up cheating the exact way she figured Cole had. Another lesson learned. *Don't date men you meet in an airport bar.*

But looking for a way out? No, she wouldn't admit to that—at least not completely. Tess thought she'd wanted more from Cole, but once she saw the buckle bunnies, she knew it was a mistake. Long-distance relationships didn't last and Cole's first love was working on his family's ranch, not living in New York City and sitting in a stuffy office building all day long. And she wouldn't think of asking him to change.

In the same regard, Tess loved her independence. She traveled around the country on business, came and went when she wanted and didn't concern herself with pleasing anyone except her cat. She had no intention of moving back to Texas. It wouldn't have worked and she was justified in leaving.

As an acquisitions analyst, Tim traveled extensively throughout the world. He'd accepted her business trips and she'd accepted his. Personal vacations were another story altogether, resulting in them never going anywhere. When Tess suggested flying home to see her family, he shot down the idea. She would have enjoyed rubbing her fiancé in Cole's face, at least once.

"If you felt that way, why didn't you pick up the phone and call me?" Tess asked. Cole pulled off the road and into a gas station. "What are you doing?"

"What does it look like? Getting gas," Cole snapped. "Why should I chase after you when you didn't stick around long enough to *ask* me what was going on? I had no reason to call. It's not like we were getting married or something."

"That'll be the day."

"Damn straight." Cole hopped from the truck and slid his credit card into the pump.

"So what, I'm not good enough to marry?" Tess shouted through the cab's open window.

How dare he think that!

Furious, Tess scampered from the truck and confronted him. Two men thinking she wasn't matrimony material in the course of one week ticked her off. "I'd make the most amazing wife!"

Tears stung her eyes, but she fought them back. She refused to allow him the satisfaction of seeing her cry. Cole took her face in his hands and drew her closer to him. She closed her eyes in anticipation of the kiss that was about to come. A kiss she didn't think she'd wanted until this very moment.

The warmth of Cole's breath on her lips heightened her unexpected desire. "I know, and don't let anyone say otherwise."

He released her, without even a peck on the cheek. Unprepared for the disappointment she felt, Tess retreated to the passenger's side of the truck. Why was it so easy for men to walk away from her? Slowly, she opened the door, uncertain if it was the gas fumes or anger that made her light-headed. Certainly, it couldn't be his rejection.

Cole finished filling the tank and slid into the seat beside her. With his hand on the ignition, he opened his mouth to speak then checked himself before the first words left his lips.

"If you have something to say to me, I'd appreciate you getting it over with so we can reach this place before lunch," Tess said.

"I promised myself I wasn't going to bring any of this up today," Cole said.

"This was your plan all along." Tess leaned against the headrest. "Confine and confront me."

Cole inhaled and exhaled slowly. Tess rolled her head to the side, expecting to see cockiness in need of an attitude adjustment. But when he shifted in his seat to face her, his pained expression puzzled her.

"You deserve better than this."

"And what *this* are you referring to? Because from where I sit, the list is getting pretty long."

"Better than a kiss in a gas station parking lot to show you how I still feel about you," Cole whispered.

"What kiss?" Tess asked.

"This one." Cole leaned across the seat and tugged

her to him. The slight firmness of his lips on hers sent a little tremble through her body, down to her toes. Warmth radiated from his mouth as the kiss deepened until she opened for him, their tongues lightly touching in unison. Cole's hand rested gently at the base of her throat while she draped her arms around his neck, urging him closer.

Thoughts swirled around each caress as she lost more of herself to him with each passing moment. Almost two years later, the familiarity of his touch and their last kiss in Vegas returned.

Dammit! That blasted city ruined everything.

Tess pushed Cole away, straightened her spine and reached for the seat belt, clicking it across her chest.

"That can't happen again." Her lips still tingled and she fought the urge to run her tongue over them. "It definitely can *never* happen again."

"At least you didn't haul off and hit me." Cole laughed.

He started the engine and headed onto the highway without further conversation. Tess dug into her bag for her sunglasses, allowing a quick glance at him. There it was—that arrogant *I got one over on her* smirk. She'd give him this one. Well, actually, she'd love to give him another one and another after that.

What are you thinking?

This wasn't going to happen. Tess refused to allow herself to fall in love with Cole again. Not that she'd been in love with him to begin with. She'd had feelings for him at one point, but she was certain those were in the past. If she knew Cole Langtry, she'd bet he was testing her with that kiss, and in that case, she wouldn't let him win.

"We're here." Cole broke into her thoughts when he

turned off the highway. A small green sign with white painted letters read Monkey Junction.

"Seriously?" Tess giggled. "This place is called Monkey Junction?"

"Sure is." Cole laughed. "Since it caters mostly to children, the name suits it. You'll understand in a minute."

There it was, larger than life, the head of a giant two-story sock monkey painted on the side of a hunter-green barn.

"Oh, my stars!" Tess jumped from the truck the moment it stopped, the shutter of her camera snapping away furiously. "I love it!"

"Morning, Cole." A man nodded as he walked past pushing a hand truck full of boxes. He was wearing a green T-shirt with a full-length sock monkey design across the front.

"Morning, Jeff," Cole said. "Is Eileen around?"

"I saw her near the office a minute or two ago."

Across the parking lot, they walked past a truck with what had to be a thousand sock monkeys stenciled on it. They really took this monkey thing to heart.

"There she is." Cole grabbed Tess's hand and pulled her in his direction. "Eileen, I want you to meet Tess, longtime friend and the web designer for our facility."

"It's a pleasure to meet you." Eileen was an attractive woman, in her late fifties with short-cropped dark hair. "Please, feel free to look around if you'd like and don't hesitate to ask if you have any questions."

"Thank you," Tess said. "Do you mind if I take some photos of your place? Oh—hello there."

A black Lab mix with short legs nudged her calf, taking her off guard.

"This is Shorty. He comes and goes around here.

Pay no mind to him and feel free to take all the photos you'd like, and Cole, if you happen to see Bingo, tell him I'm looking for him. He took off on that golf cart an hour ago and I haven't seen him since."

"Will do," Cole said.

"Why is she so nice if you're going to be the competition?" Tess asked.

"When it comes to helping people with disabilities, you can't have too many facilities, especially since we're going for our PATH International certifications. Not every place you come across is accredited. Plus it's a hundred miles between here and Bridle Dance and Eileen and Bingo are more than happy to support us and offer their expertise. They're good people."

"What's PATH International?" Tess asked.

"PATH stands for Professional Association of Therapeutic Horsemanship and the Premier Accredited Center certification will allow us to provide the best equine-assisted therapy we possibly can."

Tires crunched on the dry dirt parking lot as a faded powder-blue minivan drove up to the wheelchair accessible ramp. Cole left Tess's side, a huge smile splayed across his face. He strode to the van and slid the door open, revealing a raven-haired beauty of a child with two ponytails tied with pink bows.

"CC!" Small arms stretched out toward him while Cole bent down to unfasten her seat belt. "I can walk, CC! Watch me!"

The girl reached beside her seat and pulled out two tiny crutches with forearm supports. When she swung herself around, Tess could see that braces encased her legs up to her knees.

"Slow down, Ever." A woman came around to the

van door. "All this child's been able to prattle on about is showing you she can walk."

"Hello, Lorraine." Cole moved aside, allowing the woman to seat the girl on the floor of the minivan so her legs dangled over the edge.

"Look, CC!" With calculated precision, the child focused on Cole, who knelt down on the ground a few feet in front of her. She took one precarious step, followed by a much steadier one.

Tess covered her mouth to keep from gasping at the child's determination and pride with each small movement. The entire staff watched the girl walk toward Cole. When she finally reached him, he wrapped his arms around her, lifting her up and swinging her around.

"I'm so proud of you, sweetie." Cole hugged the girl, his eyes glassy, making Tess think a tear would spill over at any moment. "So proud."

"I wanted to call and tell you, but I was told to wait and maybe you'd be here this week so I could show you."

"Lorraine, you know you can call me anytime," Cole said. Tess figured the woman must be Ever's mother. "You still have my number, right?"

The woman nodded. "We didn't want to bother you."

Cole's eyes narrowed, and Tess guessed he held his tongue due to the child's presence. The conversation didn't seem new, but rather a familiar one.

"I want you to meet a friend of mine," Cole said. "Ever, this is Tess. Tess, meet Ever, my little cowgirl in the making."

"Hi, Tess." Ever's twilight-blue eyes sparkled when she spoke. "CC has a girlfriend."

Tess felt the heat rise to her cheeks at Ever's reference. "It's a pleasure to meet you. I'm just a friend of Cole's, though."

"And you're a girl." Ever pulled at Cole's hat until it came off his head, and placed it on top of hers, covering most of her face. "She's pretty."

"I can't argue with you there." Cole winked at Tess.

"Put me down, CC, I want to walk."

"Well, look at you, Super Girl." A woman with the name *Caitlin* embroidered on her shirt pocket approached. "Are you ready for your therapy?"

"Yes, ma'am," Ever replied. "Will you watch me?"

"I wouldn't miss it for the world," Cole said.

Tess had never seen Cole so intently fixated on someone as he was this moment with Ever. Bracing his arms on the round pen's fence rail, Cole watched the slip of a girl astride a light bay-colored mare. Ever sat absolutely straight, holding on to the two side handles on the royal blue clothlike saddle.

"This is what it's about, right here," Cole said. "This was my father's dream."

Tess saw Cole swipe at his eyes with the back of his hand, trying hard to hide his emotions. In the lifetime she'd known Cole, she couldn't remember him shedding a single tear. She wouldn't have guessed this side of him existed. The same went for his father.

"What's wrong with her?" Tess hoped her question wasn't callous.

"Ever has cerebral palsy. Up until I last saw her a little over a week ago, she was still in a wheelchair. Today is the first I've seen her walk more than a few feet without anyone supporting her."

"I didn't realize hippotherapy was that powerful." Tess had heard of the therapy but hadn't paid too much attention to it. "How can a horse teach her to walk?"

"It *allows* her to walk." Cole turned to face Tess with his arms out, palms facedown. "The horse's gait very closely mimics a human's walk."

He moved his hands up and down. "If you walk with your hands on your hips, you will feel a steady rhythm. A horse's movements are almost identical to ours. In Ever's case, she needed to strengthen her core muscles and improve her balance. Hippotherapy builds up her core and allows her to have the ability to walk with the aid of crutches. The day may come when she won't need them anymore."

"Interesting saddle." Tess noted its thinness and lack of leather.

"It allows the rider to feel the muscular movements of the horse better so they can engage the right muscles. The two separate handles are easier to grip and don't interfere with her sense of balance."

"Why does she call you CC?" Tess asked.

"It's short for Cowboy Cole. She's called me that from the moment my dad brought us here last year."

Tess watched the girl ride closer to the fence rail. Her pink top matched the tint of her cheeks. An assistant led the horse, and her therapist and another staff member flanked both sides. Cole waved his hat in the air when she passed, cheering her on. Looking around, Tess tried to find the girl's mother. A parent testimonial would be a great addition to the website.

"I don't see her mom. Did she leave?"

"Ever's in foster care," Cole said. "Has been since the day she was born."

"She's an orphan?" Tess's voice was louder than she had intended.

"Some people can't cope with raising a special-needs child," Cole said. "Ever was abandoned as part of the

Texas Safe Haven Law. Since it's anonymous, her parents' identity will remain a mystery."

"What?" Tess shook her head, unable to fathom the thought of deserting a child. How could anyone hand their child over to a stranger and not care what happened to it? "They gave her away because she has cerebral palsy?"

"Most likely, and it's not as uncommon as you might think."

If she was lucky enough to be blessed with a child, and that child was born with a disability, Tess was certain she wouldn't be able to give it away. How could you live with yourself afterward?

"People are sick." Tess spit out the words.

"Don't be too judgmental," Cole said. "We don't know the circumstances. Maybe it was a selfish socialite that didn't want the stigma of a special-needs child, but it also might have been an abused single mother, without any means to care for a child. She may have felt someone else would give her a better life. We'll never know the truth and, unfortunately, it's something Ever will always question."

"So she's a ward of the state?" Tess asked.

"Pretty much, although my family is her benefactor."

"Her benefactor?" Tess tried to process the fact that this tiny girl in front of her was treated like an object instead of a human being.

"This past spring, Ever needed new leg braces. She had outgrown her old ones and I'm sure she'll outgrow these soon. Without new braces she can't walk, but since she's in foster care, sometimes there's red tape involved in getting what she needs."

"I don't understand. You said she can't walk without them."

"She can't," Cole explained. "They not only support her, they stretch her overflexed muscles, allowing her more mobility. Without them, she's confined to a wheelchair."

"How can anyone deny her something she needs?" Tess grew more flustered by the moment. "What kind of quality of life does she have without them?"

"Calm down, Tess." Cole motioned for her to move farther away from the pen so Ever wouldn't hear their conversation when she came around. "She'd have gotten them eventually, but there was no telling if it would take a week or a month. My father wanted to take control of the situation and speed the process up, so he stepped in and became her benefactor."

"Why didn't your parents adopt her?"

"Because they're over the age limit. Honestly, I thought of it myself, but a single male can send up some warning flags. Ever is one of thousands of children with disabilities available for adoption. Those big blue eyes are the sole reason my father wanted to build the hippotherapy facility."

"So children like her can be provided for." Tess narrowed her gaze. "I'm going to bust your brothers right in the nose."

"Whoa." Cole laughed. "Easy there, slugger."

"Have Chase and Shane been out here?" Tess waved when Ever rode by on her horse. "You're doing great!"

"That's my rodeo princess!" Cole strode back to the fence. "Yes, and they have no problem being her benefactor, but they feel there are enough hippotherapy centers in the state and don't want to build another one."

"But you said there isn't one for a hundred miles." The realization of the situation suddenly hit Tess. "It comes down to money, doesn't it?"

"There isn't another PATH International facility around for a hundred miles and yes, their decision's money propelled. You earn more with a rodeo school than you do with a nonprofit. They only see the bottom line, not who it benefits."

"We have to change their minds, Cole."

"That's exactly what I was hoping you'd say."

Chapter Four

Tess didn't hear her mother leave the house, but she'd bet Maggie was up and out shortly after Tess called it a night. The sun peeked over the horizon, gently waking the songbirds from their slumber. After a few hours of sleep, she enjoyed the brief walk into town, even in the briskness of the fall air, strolling past a few cemetery-filled front lawns all ready for Halloween. No matter the time of day, or spooky decorations, Ramblewood felt safe and secure. A foreign concept in her five-story New York City walk-up.

Light spilled onto Main Street through the luncheonette's picture window, casting shadows of magpies on the sidewalk. Outside, Tess watched her mother and Bridgett bustle through their morning routines. The casual gestures her mother made toward Bridgett made Tess yearn for the same closeness. A stranger would assume Bridgett was Maggie's daughter by their ease and camaraderie.

"Tess, this is a surprise." Maggie hefted a tray of pies onto her shoulder, carrying them to the display case near the front window. "You got in so late, I figured you'd sleep through to afternoon. Did you and Cole have a good time yesterday?"

"Cole, huh?" Bridgett peered through the kitchen opening. "Do tell! Especially since you never showed at Slater's."

"I don't want to hear any dirty details," Bert said. "You leave those parts out, you hear?"

"Put your tongues back in your mouths." Tess fixed herself a cup of coffee. "I was out at the ranch working with Kay on some marketing ideas and Cole wasn't even around. One of the mares was foaling and he was in the barn. I hate to break it to you, but there was nothing salacious going on."

Bridgett's shoulders visibly slumped. "And here I thought I could live vicariously through you."

"Not when it comes to Cole Langtry, you won't," Tess said. Unless you counted the impromptu kiss in the gas station parking lot.

Tess considered herself the good Girl Scout and was prepared for most things in life. But for some reason, Cole's kisses managed to take her off guard. It was one thing when they were kids, but as an adult, he shouldn't have this much of an effect on her. If she closed her eyes she could still feel the heat of his body inside the truck's cab. "Oh, this is ridiculous!"

"You look like a snake bit you on the toe." Bridgett whispered through the kitchen pass-through, "What are you hiding?"

"Nothing you need to concern yourself with." Bert's head popped out. "Stop gossiping and finish slicing those lemons or else we won't be ready in time to open."

Bridgett mouthed, *Tell me later,* to Tess before she returned to work.

"Mom, I met the most amazing—"

"One second, dear." Maggie pushed through the swinging door of the kitchen, returning immediately with another tray. She motioned around the room with her free arm. "Can you straighten out those chairs, please? We'll have a full house in a few."

Tess aligned the vinyl-covered stainless steel chairs while her mother ducked behind the counter for a rag and made one more pass over the Formica surface for good measure.

"Bridgett, add tomato bisque to the Specials Board. I'm going to start a batch in a minute." Maggie didn't bother to look up. "I'm sorry, Tess, what was it you were saying?"

"It can wait."

For some reason she felt a conversation that involved Ever deserved more of her mother's attention. Tess had hoped to make the best of this trip, visit with family, catch up with a few friends, attend the wedding and head home to New York. Already her plans were shifting since Kay had asked her to help market Dance of Hope.

Despite what happened with Cole a few years ago, he didn't seem to hold much of a grudge, although she wouldn't blame him if he never spoke to her again after being a no-show at his father's funeral.

Why did he have to kiss me and confuse the issue?

"I should have come home for the funeral," Tess said, louder than she anticipated.

"Yes, you should have." Maggie stopped long enough to lay a hand over her daughter's. "But what's done is done. You can't go back."

"No, I can't." The words had more than one meaning, but luckily her mother didn't catch on. Tess wasn't ready to admit she was contemplating a move back home for fear everyone, especially her parents, would think she'd failed in the big city.

Tess was tired of running through the million *what-ifs* that had plagued her since her tidy little world came crashing down. What if she'd taken on more accounts at work, even though her workload was almost unbearable? What if she'd been more of a team player, although she always worked well with Cheryl-Leigh? So why was her roommate still there and Tess out of a job?

Cheryl-Leigh knew Tess was vying for a promotion and even supported her bid by offering to help in any way she could. While Tess was grateful for her friend's support, she couldn't help but wonder if her help was Tess's downfall. There was no question about Tess's ability to get the job done, but from an outsider's perspective, Cheryl-Leigh was the one always lending a helping hand, which made it look like Tess was unable to manage on her own. Was it intentional on Cheryl-Leigh's part or was she reading too much into it?

"Mom, where are all the napkin dispensers?" Tess looked around the luncheonette.

"I completely forgot I polished them last night. They're behind the counter at the end. Don't get them all smudgy with your fingerprints, though."

"Am I supposed to wear gloves?" Tess teased, causing Bridgett to snicker.

"Here." Maggie thrust a pair of disposable latex gloves at Tess as she walked past.

"I guess so." Pulling them on, Tess began to set out a dispenser on each table.

Seeing her reflection in the side of the shiny chrome, Tess considered herself reasonably attractive. Which left her once again questioning what went wrong with Tim? If she'd gone on that last business trip with him he wouldn't have returned married, although the logical side of her brain reasoned that since he did, he must have been having an affair for a while.

Tess glanced around. She'd missed the unpretentious and homey surroundings of the luncheonette. Trophies and photographs from Maggie's Silkie Chicken competition days sat on a shelf above the kitchen pass-through window. It was a quirky little eatery, and her mother took pride in every square foot of it.

Years of hard work had paid off and Maggie had something tangible to show for it. Tess wasn't able to say the same. Sure, she worked hard and had created some very successful websites, but at the end of the day, what did she physically have to hold in her hand? The key to the front door of the Magpie meant more to Maggie than the fanciest of jewelry.

Not one to sit idle, Tess scrolled down her list of things to do on her smartphone. She sent out a few résumés at the touch of a button. At least she'd be able to remain in constant contact with the industry and a few headhunters both in New York and in nearby Austin and San Antonio while she was here.

The thought of opening her open web design business in Ramblewood crossed her mind. But with most small businesses easily able to create their own marketing online for far less than she would charge, Tess didn't think it was the most prudent choice.

She'd always prided herself on knowing the next step, so this newfound lack of direction really threw Tess. She slipped the phone in her pocket and started refilling the glass sugar dispensers Bridgett lined up on the counter.

Her problems in New York seemed so trivial after meeting Ever. From the moment Tess left Monkey Junction with Cole, Ever had consumed most of her thoughts. When she'd returned home from Bridle Dance last night, she'd researched cerebral palsy and hippotherapy until her eyes no longer stayed open. The sheer number of special-needs children placed for adoption throughout the country overwhelmed her.

From her own research and the information Cole had shared with her, Tess concluded that Ever had a form of spastic diparesis cerebral palsy, in which the muscles of her legs wouldn't relax. Her upper body didn't seem affected, at least not that Tess noticed.

"What was it you wanted to tell me, dear?" Maggie wiped down the soda dispenser. "Better yet, come tell me in the kitchen while I start the tomato bisque."

"I met the sweetest girl named Ever at the hippotherapy facility yesterday." Tess followed her mother into the pantry, grabbing the large soup pot while Maggie gathered the ingredients. As she spoke, Tess was unable to keep a lid on her admiration for the little girl. "I've never seen anyone with such fierce determination in my life."

"Kay adores her." Maggie peered around the pantry door when the front door bells jingled and Beau Bradley walked in. "Poor child, though. I heard she has it pretty rough."

"From what I hear, she's steadily improving." Tess set a large wooden spoon next to the range. "I can't understand why anyone would give her up for adoption because she has cerebral palsy."

"Some people don't want that responsibility, Tess, but it doesn't make them a bad person."

Yesterday Cole had told her about Ever's extensive physical therapy, and, thanks to his father's generous funding, the little girl had access to the best neurologists in the state. Hearing what Ever had gone through in her short lifetime pained Tess, and knowledge of the child's abandonment made it even more heart-wrenching. No child deserved to suffer emotionally or physically.

After meeting Ever, she understood why Joe had taken such a liking to the girl. She was easy to fall in love with and her strength was amazing. Not once did Tess hear her say she couldn't do something. She might struggle, but Ever squinted her eyes as if sizing up an imaginary foe and put a hundred and ten percent effort into it.

"Is it Ever or Cole that has you so distracted this morning?" Maggie asked after she returned from taking Beau's order.

"I can assure you, Cole is the furthest thing from my mind," Tess fibbed. His kiss was still twirling around in her memory. "I'm almost speechless when it comes to Ever. I'm in awe of that child."

Tess had strived for independence and success from an early age and she saw a lot of herself in Ever, appreciating the girl's tenacity and fearlessness. With that drive and spirit, there was nothing Ever couldn't overcome.

"From what I've heard, she's a remarkable little girl." Maggie pulled a pencil from behind her ear, an order pad from her apron pocket and approached the swinging door. "You'll have to tell me more about her later. Bert, can you keep an eye on the bisque for me?"

Tess followed her mother out of the kitchen. Bridgett bounced from table to table, coffeepot in hand. Her ginger-hued mane was pulled high on her crown, cascading into ringlets between her shoulder blades. Long lean legs crossed the room in mere seconds. In her pink-and-white ruffled uniform, she reminded Tess of a circus pony, prancing through a ring of obstacles with precision. She belonged onstage somewhere, not waiting tables in a small town, but Bridgett was content with the status quo.

Given the busyness of the morning rush, Tess grabbed an apron and tied it around her waist. Maggie's hesitation to hire another waitress still baffled Tess. Even though her mother had reduced the Magpie's hours to only serve breakfast and lunch, Tess and her father argued that Maggie still needed help, but Maggie was certain she'd be able to handle it.

"Thank you, dear." Maggie brushed past her. "We're really packing them in today."

"Don't you every day?" Tess's question fell on deaf ears.

Stubbornness was a hereditary trait. Grabbing plastic water glasses from the shelf, Tess bent down to open the large ice maker and saw that some of her magnets adorned the front.

Sliding the chest door closed, she noticed the ashtray she'd crafted in summer camp next to the antique cash register, serving as a need-one, take-one penny holder. Looking around the luncheonette, she recognized a part of herself in every corner. Ever wouldn't experience that feeling of belonging until someone adopted her. She wouldn't be able to visit her childhood home, filled with love and family.

"You haven't forgotten a thing," Bridgett said, when the doors closed at three. "Thanks for the help today."

"It's been a while since I did this in high school," Tess said. "Not much has changed, not even Bert's cooking."

"I heard that, little lady," Bert hollered from beyond the kitchen wall.

Tess helped Bridgett and Maggie wash the floor and prep for the following day. She wasn't used to working on her feet for so many hours and wasn't sure she'd be able to hold out much longer in her thin-soled Keds. Even her toes ached.

"You're coming to Slater's later, right?" Bridgett asked over her shoulder. "Since you stood me up last night."

"I'll have to talk to my feet and get back to you." Tess perched on the edge of the stool. "Plus, I kind of wanted to work on the website a little more, considering I didn't do anything with it today."

As Bridgett left for the night, a look passed between Bridgett and Maggie that Tess normally would question, but she was too tired to give it a second thought. Forcing herself to stand, she immediately regretted walking into town instead of driving.

"Tess dear, I could really use your help. I have an order for three Kentucky Sky-High pies for tonight." Her mother moved toward the stairs leading to the upstairs office. "There's some piecrust resting in the fridge. Whip them up for me because I have to go over the books tonight for the accountant."

"Mother, I haven't made one of those pies since I was twelve." There was no way Tess could possibly make one pie, let alone three. She couldn't even remember the ingredients.

"The ovens are already preheating. Don't worry, it will come back to you, like waiting tables did. You know you could always work here until you found something else," her mother said before disappearing up the stairs, not giving Tess a chance to respond.

Tess looked around the kitchen for pie-making equipment. Finding none, she made her way to the stockroom. Stainless steel racks lined the walls, their shelves laden with pots, pans, mixers and every other possible kitchen gadget known to man. Taking a stack of well-worn pie tins, Tess scanned the pantry walls for ingredients, trying to remember what went into chocolate-pecan pie. Pecans and chocolate were a given. Sugar, too. Was it molasses or corn syrup? She picked up both bottles and held them at eye level.

"Molasses!" She returned the corn syrup to the shelf. "Definitely molasses."

She removed the piecrust and eggs from the walk-in fridge.

"Okay, Tess," she said to herself. "You've gotten this far, let's figure the rest out."

She rolled out the crusts for each tin and lined the bottoms of the dishes very generously with pecans. Unwrapping the large brick of chocolate, she chose a cleaver from the wall-mounted magnetic knife rack and began to chop it into small chunks. After tossing the chocolate chunks with a little flour, she heaped it on top of the pecans. Staring at the eggs, she attempted to remember how many to use, silently cursing the fact her mother had never written down a recipe in her entire life.

"It was threes! Three eggs, three tablespoons butter, three teaspoons vanilla, a third of a cup of molasses," she sang, recalling how her mother made the recipe simple by using three for all the measurements.

Proud of herself, she mixed three separate batches of pie filling, not wanting to chance one large batter. Recipes invariably came out wrong when she doubled or tripled them. There was always too much or too little of something.

The urge to lick the spoon before she tossed it in the sink proved too great. No one was watching and who in their right mind would pass up the sweetness of the

Kentucky Sky-High batter. Besides, she had to insure it was edible.

The pies in the oven and a timer set to an hour, Tess spun around, giddy and smiling, lifting her apron high in the air like she used to as a little girl. Mom was right, it had come back to her.

"Well." A deep, sensual voice spoke from behind her. "What do we have here?"

"Cole!" Tess smoothed her apron down in front of her. "You really need to stop sneaking up on me."

"Why? It's fun." He tore a paper towel off the holder and strode to the sink to wet it. Cupping her chin, he dabbed at the side of her mouth and smiled. "Someone's been licking the spoon."

"I can do that myself, thank you." Tess swatted him away. "Did you come here to harass me?"

"No, but if you have a minute I wanted to run a few ideas for the ranch past you."

Tess looked at the kitchen timer. "How do fifty-one minutes sound?"

Flashbacks flooded Cole's memory like a movie-clip montage at an awards ceremony. Birthday parties, year-end exam study sessions, decorating cookies for fundraisers—all within the walls of the Magpie. They may be older, but that familiar feeling returned when they sat side by side at the counter, their bodies barely touching.

"I have so many ideas for Dance of Hope." Tess glanced over her notes. "Have you eaten—because I'm starving right now. Those pies made me crave a salad."

"I'm not even going to ask the logic on that one, but if you're going to make one, I could eat."

"Come join me in the kitchen." Tess motioned for him to follow. "Can you grab my notepad, too?"

Mesmerized by the speed at which she julienned the carrots, Cole watched Tess prepare a lavish chef's salad. They sat at the kitchen worktable and ate while Tess continued to loosely sketch website concepts. The gentle fluidity of her hand as she drew beckoned him to kiss the inside of her wrist, trailing up her arm—

"Are you listening to me?"

"Sure am, darling," Cole drawled.

The timer in the kitchen rang and Tess jumped up. *Saved by the bell.*

"Let me get these out of the oven."

Cole stood alongside the stainless steel counter of the kitchen watching her test the pie's center with a knife and then place each one on a rack to cool.

"I think we need to contact the newspapers, television and radio stations. It's never too soon to raise public awareness and interest in the project by organizing an annual fund-raiser for the facility," she called back over her shoulder.

"Whoa." Tess's words began to register. "You're getting ahead of yourself. I need you to help me convince Shane and Chase to sign off on the therapy facility first. We can't run amok and announce this across town. I need their approval before we launch a media campaign like that."

"Then what am I doing here?" Tess asked. "If your brothers see the public's interest, they might be swayed to change their mind. But please, don't tell me we *can't* do something. We need to make it happen."

"This was my father's dream and I *will* see it through." Cole folded his arms defensively. "I eat, sleep and breathe this project. This battle has torn my family in two, but you have to realize this isn't just up to me. This is a corporation we are dealing with. Major financial decisions require a majority vote, Tess. My hands are tied on certain things and this constant forward motion my mom keeps pushing is why Shane keeps running to your father."

"Untie them." Tess sat before him on one of the stools, placing her hands on his knees. "Bend the rules. Hell, break the rules if that's what it takes, but don't say you can't do something. Do you think Ever allows anything to get in her way?"

The corners of Tess's mouth lifted when she mentioned Ever's name. Cole knew Tess was right. The miniature cowgirl looked up to him when in fact he admired her grit more than anyone else's. The most frustrating part of the entire situation was that when his brothers blocked the facility, they blocked people like Ever from getting a potentially life-changing therapy. The benefits far outweighed the cost and it hurt more than any bull toss in the rodeo ring that they didn't see it that way.

"I won't fail." Cole stood and broke away from the searing heat of Tess's hands atop his thighs. The woman was centimeters from heading into dangerous territory and luckily his frustration cooled the flames of his desire. "We need to be smart and not ruffle too many feathers or else your father will haul me into court."

"For the record, my dad's not happy to be in the middle of this. Coexecutor or not, I think he was hoping everyone would work it out before he had to step in. Legally he must enforce the will."

"I know, and I wish my father hadn't complicated matters by naming a coexecutor, but Mom claims she was all right with the idea when the will was drafted. She didn't want to handle the business side, so this made sense to her. That's not to say she wasn't devastated when she heard Shane ran to your father like a little tattletale."

Given the friendship Henry and his father had shared, Shane's announcement had almost knocked Cole out of his boots. Especially when he considered Henry was the one who set up the nonprofit license for their father. Cole knew this put Henry in a difficult position and one their father couldn't have anticipated. Shane and Chase's actions were pitting friends and neighbors against one another, but dollar signs mattered most to them.

"I wish there was something I could do to help," Tess said.

"There is." Cole stood. "You can box up these pies. We'll let them cool in the car on the way over."

Tess let out one of the snarky little snorts she'd developed as a child. The same laugh he'd made fun of when they were growing up.

"Those pies are for one of my mom's customers." Tess tapped at the pad. "You and I have plenty of work to do."

"I'm the customer." Cole loved watching her face turn from sarcastic to confused. "Come with me."

"My mother knew this, didn't she?" Tess placed her hands on her hips in a defensive stance.

"She sure did." Cole chuckled. "Let's get a move on before you're late for your own welcome-home party."

"Wait. You have to promise to do something for me." Tess chewed her inner cheek, puckering her lips like a man shaving one side of his face. It was a cute habit she'd never outgrown and one Cole didn't even think she was aware of.

"Depends." Cole knew better than to give her full rein with anything. "What do you want?"

"Ever's hippotherapy schedule." Tess squared her shoulders, bracing for some form of argument.

"Okay."

"Okay? That's it?" Tess appeared leery he'd let her off the hook that easy.

"She's addictive, isn't she?" Cole knew the tiny tike's power. "Ever was someone I instantly recognized as special."

Joe had met Ever when he'd donated a few older horses to Monkey Junction. Immediately charmed, he urged Kay and the rest of the family to get to know her. The first day Cole had seen the little girl with the unusual name astride one of the hippotherapy horses in her blue chest protector and riding helmet held a special place in his heart. Cole and his brothers visited when they could, but it was Joe and Kay who spent the majority of the time there.

With more spirit than any of the horses they trained, Ever had the ability to turn a bad day into one you were thankful for. And Cole often thought if he were married, he'd adopt Ever himself. His heart ached knowing someone had given this precious child away. He hoped her birth parents intended for her to have a better life, because he'd never comprehend how someone couldn't love that precious girl.

"Yes, now are you happy?" Tess asked. "She's had the same effect on me and I would like to spend more time with her. Can you arrange it?"

"I can do you one better, I'll drive you out to see her whenever you like." It was a tall order, considering Chase and Shane's sporadic appearances at the family ranch. Cole was still learning the business side of Bridle Dance and the logistics of the sod farm, while trying to run the breeding program at the same time.

Even tonight he knew he should be at home running through their artificial insemination schedule for the mares, but he was finding it difficult to stay away from Tess. He trusted Lexi Lawson, the ranch's equine veterinarian, and he was grateful for her team's help, but he still needed to keep on top of things.

Cole drove Tess to her house so she could quickly shower off the day's restaurant grime. An hour later, they rolled into the bar's gravel parking lot. The lights were dim when they entered Slater's Mill, but bright enough to see across the well-worn hardwood dance floor. Lexi, Bridgett and Cole's cousin Brandon Slater sat in the large round booth they usually occupied. Brandon's wife, Vicki, pushed four-month-old Randi Lynn back and forth in a stroller with her foot while she perched on the end of the booth. His uncle Charlie, the Mill's owner, waved from behind the bar then continued to talk with Shane.

"Tess! Cole!" Bridgett jumped out of the booth. "Let me get those for you."

Bridgett took the pies from Tess and placed them on the table. Lifting the lid, she peeked inside. "Yum! Maggie outdid herself this time."

"Not Maggie." Cole wrapped his arm around Tess and gave her a quick squeeze. "This one here is responsible."

"I had a sneaking suspicion Maggie was going to con you into baking the pies." Bridgett laughed. "Let me go grab some plates."

"Tess, it's been ages!" Vicki stood and gave her friend a hug. Cole instantly hated relinquishing Tess, enjoying the feel of her body against his. A cold shower was definitely in order when he got home.

"You look amazing," Tess said. "And your daughter is so beautiful."

"She takes after her mom." Brandon leaned in to Tess. "Good to have you home."

"Thank you." Tess squatted down beside the napping infant. "How does she sleep through the noise?"

"Little baby earmuffs." Vicki grinned, moving Randi Lynn's hoodie aside to reveal a tiny pink headset. "We can't stay long. Soon this place will get so crowded that you'll have to go outside to change your mind. But we wanted to throw you a little welcome-home get-together. A few of us are meeting tomorrow out at Bridle Dance to work on some of the favors for Miranda's bridal shower and I know Mable would love to see you."

"Sure. I told Kay I would be out there first thing," Tess said. "Are Miranda and Jesse coming tonight?"

"They won't get back from San Antonio until late," Lexi said. "Last-minute wedding preparations."

Tess directed her attention to the stroller. "She looks like a little angel."

Cole had never seen Tess take an interest in children before.

"That she is," Vicki said. "And she certainly came into this world full force, and fashionably late for the party, no less."

"My mom said she was born at Double Trouble." Tess smiled when Randi Lynn yawned and lifted a tiny hand to hers.

"And the place certainly lived up to its name." Vicki recounted the day her daughter was born on a shower curtain liner at the ranch Cole's future sister-in-law, Miranda, owned. "I barely made it through her baby shower when this little one decided to join the fun."

Tess never took her eyes off Randi Lynn, holding

fast to her tiny hand as she listened to Vicki and Brandon tell the story. For a brief moment, Cole imagined being married to Tess, with Ever as their daughter and maybe a few more children playing around. It was a fleeting fantasy, though, as more people came over to say hello to Tess.

The woman was gone for a couple of years and suddenly she was a celebrity. He'd wager her two-year absence had more to do with her ex-fiancé than it did with their breakup. Tess had always made it home for the holidays, but once Tim entered her life, she didn't step foot back in town.

"Earth to Cole." Bridgett waved her hand in front of his face. "I said your uncle Charlie wants to talk to you. He wants to know how your mom is doing."

"Well, then he can get his butt over to the house and visit his sister instead of always going through me. Shane's sitting right there. Why doesn't he ask him?"

"Whoa, don't shoot the messenger," Brandon said. "You know how my dad is. He feels awkward and doesn't know what to say. He doesn't handle grief very well, and in all fairness, he did go to visit her a lot in the beginning. We'd like to see your mom get off the ranch every once in a while."

Cole knew his cousin was right. His mother was spending all her time on Bridle Dance, only leaving to go grocery shopping, and even then, she bought enough to last a week or more.

From across the room, Shane sat at the bar and watched the group. Cole hated the tension in his family and knew his mother was in a constant state of distress over the situation. No one had expected Joe to leave the ranch to anyone other than Kay.

Flattering as it was, Cole wished his father's will

had bequeathed everything to her. In time, he knew it would have come down to this exact situation anyway and he reckoned that was his father's reason for doing it—so his mother wouldn't have to. But it sure didn't make things any easier when they could barely stand to be in the same room together.

Shane's body stiffened. Turning, Cole saw his youngest brother, Chase, lift Tess in the air and swing her around. Home a day early. Cole suspected he didn't have a good ride in Daly City.

"Would you look at you, pretty lady," Chase said. "It sure took you long enough to find your way back to us. We've missed you, girl."

Chase might be against building a hippotherapy facility, but he obviously didn't hold anything against Tess for not coming home for the funeral. Shane slammed his beer bottle down on the bar and Cole would bet his last dollar that was steam coming out of his brother's ears when he stormed out the door.

"You better save a dance for me tonight," Tess said. "I'm getting my second wind."

"Think you can remember how?" Chase teased.

"It hasn't been that long." Tess playfully pushed against his shoulder. "Who knows, I may even teach you a thing or two out there. We have line dancing in New York, you know."

The exchange between Tess and Chase gave Cole an idea. With her persuasive charm and his brother's all-forgiving nature, Tess might be able to convince Chase to vote his twenty-five percent in Cole's direction, making her much more useful than he expected.

Chapter Five

"Good morning." Tess looked up from her laptop when Cole shuffled into the kitchen. "I'm so glad the ranch has Wi-Fi now. It makes my job much easier."

Shirtless, barefoot and with his jeans half-unzipped, Cole looked around the room in bewilderment. And damn if he wasn't sexy, even with his unruly hair standing up at odd angles.

"What?" Cole scratched at his rib cage.

"Good heavens." Tess fought to keep her jaw from banging against the table at the raw sight of him. "Wi-Fi—glad you—uh, have an internet connection."

"Oh, that. Dad couldn't live without it. Mom said he was more in love with his iPhone than he was with her. One night when he was fiddling with it at the table, she told him if his phone was so smart it could cook for him from now on and then fed his dinner to the garbage disposal."

"I can picture that." Tess laughed, focusing her attention on the screen and not the half-naked man before her. "I have the domain name secured."

"You have a what secured?" Cole asked gruffly, drawing her attention to him once again. Then he held up his hand. "Better yet, don't tell me. Why are you here so early anyway? And why does it look like you've been here for hours? The sun's barely up."

"Because I told your mom I would and I've only been here for thirty minutes." Tess quietly snickered. "Since when do you sleep in? I thought you ranchers were up before the chickens. Your mom is already dressed and out in the garden. Come here so I can go over this with you."

"Gimme a minute." Cole poured himself a mug of coffee, topped off hers and grabbed an ice cube before joining her at the table. Tess looked up at him when he plopped it into her mug. "I may not know what domain names are or whatever it is you're *securing,* but I do remember how you drink your coffee."

"Thank you." Tess took a sip of the brew. "I should have a basic site up and running by the end of the day. But I need a bank account for the donations and a non-profit license."

"And she rattles on before I even swallow." Cole raked his hand through his hair, shifting in his chair. "I have to call Jon regarding the nonprofit. Your father has that paperwork and I believe everything is filed and in order, but I don't know where anything stands anymore since your father's coexecutor of the estate. Shane's already told him we're going against the will."

Despite giving him a hard time, Tess admired and respected the man before her. The oldest of the Langtry boys had become the family patriarch of sorts. The success or failure of the ranch started by his great-grandparents lay squarely on his shoulders. The extra creases across his forehead were likely carved from the anxiety of added responsibilities and a fear of failure. She knew the past few months had been a major adjustment for the family. She was also beginning to realize every day was a constant battle for him.

Tess knew something more was bothering Cole by the way he avoided eye contact. Her father's old saying came to mind—*You can tell a lot about a man by the look in his eyes. If you can't see his eyes, there's something he doesn't want you to know.*

"All right." Tess closed the lid on her laptop, giving Cole her full attention. "More's going on here besides this issue with Shane. Let's hear it."

Cole rose from the table, looking out over Kay's massive vegetable garden. His broad shoulders tensed then dropped for a split second. Inhaling deeply, he turned to face her.

"I need you to do me a favor," Cole said. "But hear me out before you get mad at me for asking."

"All right." Tess stiffened, almost afraid to hear his request. "This should be interesting."

"You seem to have a pretty good rapport with Chase." Cole slid into the chair beside her and lowered his voice to the point where Tess had to lean in closer to hear what he was saying. "I don't think Shane will loosen his grip on the rodeo school idea but Chase might, with the right persuasion."

Cole clasped her hands tightly between his. He parted his lips slightly, less than a foot away from hers, when suddenly Tess realized what he was asking of her. She tried to move back but his hands were like vise grips on hers.

"Eww, are you asking me to come on to your brother?" Tess wrinkled up her nose.

"No, but a little flirtation wouldn't hurt." Cole sheepishly looked down at his feet. "Especially if it means people like Ever would have a better shot at life."

Tess kicked his bare feet, causing him to release his hold on her. "That's pretty low, even for you."

"Ouch, Tess!" Cole rubbed his toes. "I don't appreciate you implying that I'm using Ever. I've loved that child from the moment I laid eyes on her. Without this facility, people—children especially—in Ever's condition may not receive the help they desperately need. That little girl couldn't walk a few months ago! Monkey Junction can't accommodate everyone and people don't have time to make the three-hour round trip from this area."

"What makes you think he'll listen to anything I have to say?"

"Because you obviously have a good relationship and I saw you two dancing last night. He doesn't appear to hold your self-imposed absence against you."

"Cole Langtry." Tess didn't think she'd live to see the day another man would ruffle his feathers. "I do believe you're jealous."

"Of Chase?" Cole smirked while avoiding her gaze. "Hardly."

"I hate to burst your bubble, but I tried talking to him last night and he made it clear the topic was off-limits."

Cole sank back against the chair. Lifting his eyes to meet hers, he said, "I don't know what else to do. One of them has to budge and I'd bet my life it won't be Shane."

"All right," Tess relented. "What do you want me to say to him?"

"Grab a bite to eat or go for a ride on one of the trails together. Talk to him, Tess, and assure him this decision will change the lives of so many people. I want this, Tess—to honor my father, Ever and everyone else in need. This *will* happen and nothing's going to stop me."

"Wow." Tess moved farther away from him. "I never

thought I'd see the day you turned into your father. Didn't what happened with Jesse teach you a lesson? You can't control every situation. What is all this constant bickering doing to your mother?"

"She's up at odd hours during the night, to the point I can't even tell when she sleeps anymore." Cole squeezed the bridge of his nose between his thumb and forefinger. "Thankfully, the wedding has given her something positive to look forward to, but what happens when that's over with? At this point, the one thing the four of us can agree on is leaving Mom out of it."

"Obviously you're failing if she's not sleeping."

"I need you." Cole placed his hands on Tess's shoulder, sending a slight tingle through her body. "You said you would help me yesterday and I'm asking you to honor that commitment."

Before Tess could respond, Cole strode from the room. She heard his footfalls on the circular staircase off the mudroom moments later. Unwilling to allow him to make her lose focus on the job Kay asked her to do, she continued to work at the kitchen table for the next few hours.

She was willing to talk to Chase, but if he wouldn't listen to her last night, she didn't know why he would today. Deciding to stretch her legs a bit, she padded through the house and attempted to wrap her head around the cyclone she'd been thrust into.

Black-and-white prints of the entire Langtry and Slater families lined the walls. Photography was Joe's passion and he had owned every camera known to man. Tess wondered if the dark room was still set up in the corner room of the cellar.

Photos of the boys through the years took precedence, but a small section was devoted to Kay Slater and Joe Langtry when they eloped to St. Louis. Joe met Kay on a cattle drive and told her it was now or never. Against her father's wishes, Kay ran away with her cowboy and they lived their happily ever after. Raising four handsome boys in this home became their legacy.

Tess still felt Joe's presence in the house—from the hand-turned legs on the kitchen table he built for their twenty-fifth wedding anniversary to the jewelry Kay religiously wore on her wrists, made from leftover nickel and silver brazing rods when the house was constructed. Memories of the man overflowed from every corner and Tess imagined how difficult it must be for Kay to lose the husband she'd loved so dearly.

Tess found Kay in the so-called vegetable garden at the side of the house. The term was used loosely since the backyard more closely resembled the Garden of Eden. Apple and pear trees framed the large parcel of land, separating it from the Tuscan-tiled pool behind the house. A large white antique greenhouse dating back to the 1900s stood immediately to the right of the area. Joe had had the steel structure restored and reconstructed after he found it lying in pieces on a neighboring ranch.

Rows of Swiss chard, cilantro, jalapeño and black cherry tomatoes were ready to be picked and used for the wedding reception. Other freshly turned rows awaited their plantings.

Kay emerged from the greenhouse with a long tray full of tiny seedlings.

"Oh, good." She motioned to Tess. "Will you help me for a moment and grab the crate of jelly jars from the porch?"

Tess set the wooden box on the potting table alongside an oblong aluminum washtub of dirt with trowels sticking out of it.

"These are favors for Miranda's bridal shower," Kay said. "Fill each jar with potting soil, leaving enough room for me to plant the herbs. We have basil, parsley, peppermint, dill and chives. I did the labels that we'll stick on afterward in calligraphy and then we'll top the jars off with ribbon and be set to go."

"You're so clever, I wouldn't have thought of this."

"Hardly." Kay laughed. "My hobbies pale in comparison to the website you're designing for us. I couldn't dream up a fraction of the things you've done."

"That's my job," Tess said. "I design elaborate sites for a living."

"And this is my job." Kay looked around the garden. "Have you seen the mouths I have to feed around here? Those boys can really pack it away. Why should I buy produce when I have this land to grow my own on? There's a reason for the Langtry money—we don't waste it on buying things when we can use what's around us. But I will say, maintaining this is starting to be a little much. I might downsize a bit next year so I can focus more on the winery. It was a hobby at first, but it has some real potential. I especially love the wine tastings."

"Why don't you have the boys help you?"

Kay laughed heartily. "Those boys know horses and cattle. They don't know one end of a hoe from the other. Then again, judging by some of the gold diggers they've brought home, maybe they do. Present company excluded, of course. But that Sharon that Shane hooked up with years ago was the worst. Lexi still hasn't forgiven him for that. Not that I blame her."

Tess nodded, remembering how heartbroken Lexi was when she returned home from college for the holidays and learned Shane had not only cheated on her, but his shotgun wedding to Sharon was planned for the following day. Their divorce came equally as fast when it turned out the baby wasn't his. Unfortunately, by the time Shane discovered the truth, he'd already grown attached to the child, making it that much harder to give him up. Now, anything akin to a serious commitment sent that man running faster than a bull out of a chute.

"Besides, I wouldn't know what to do with myself if I didn't have this to piddle around in."

"It's larger than I ever remembered it being."

"I expanded it this past spring, before Joe died." Kay's voice trailed off. "I had the idea to sell produce to some of the local restaurants, but with the wedding coming up, it's a race to get everything done. It was too much to take on."

"I can't believe Jesse's getting married." Tess tried to steer the conversation onto a happier subject. "It seems like yesterday we were playing cowboys and Indians around the ranch."

"You kids shot up so fast," Kay said. "Miranda's a great girl, hails from Washington, D.C. I think you'll really like her. She's a feisty one and exactly what Jesse needs."

Tess worked alongside Kay, listening to stories involving the Langtry men, some old, some she hadn't heard before. But during the conversation, she realized how much being a family meant to Kay and how pained she was that her sons were at odds with one another.

"I don't know what happened between you and Cole," Kay said, adding water to the peppermint she'd planted. "I don't need to, either, but any fool can see it's eating away at the two of you and you're both at fault for letting it go on too long. I'll tell you a very valuable lesson I've learned over this past year. Life can change

in the blink of an eye, and when it does, there are no
I'm sorrys or I should've saids or shouldn't have saids.
By that time, it's too late. There were many things I
wish I'd said to Joe before he died and I'll never have
that chance again. Life is short, Tess."

Kay reached for the parsley and gently placed it inside a jelly jar, her haunting words echoing in Tess's
head.

"Well, honey child, let me look at you!" Mable scut-
tled down the side porch stairs, her apple cheeks glow-
ing. "We need to fatten you up a bit."

Tess wrapped her arms around Mable, allowing herself to enjoy the warmth of the woman who took everyone under her wing. Mable Promise, Double Trouble's
house manager, caretaker and mother to all, was the
happiest person Tess knew. No matter how bleak things
were, even her husband's own illness and death, she
found the bright side. And today she smelled strongly
of cinnamon, which Tess hoped meant one thing.

"You made cinnamon rolls this morning, didn't
you?" Tess whispered in the older woman's ear. "Any
chance you brought some with you? I love them more
than my mom's but don't tell her."

"I heard that." Maggie stood on the porch beside
Vicki Slater. "And I'll have to agree with you, Mable's
cinnamon rolls do deserve the blue ribbon."

Inside, the women gathered around the large butcher-
block island of the Langtry kitchen. Vicki lifted the
cover off a shallow, rectangular box and removed sheets
of heavy white and ecru paper. From a small paper bag,
she laid out a handful of tools.

"I had the most delightful bridal shower idea." Petite
and perky, the former head cheerleader with the naturally blond hair and bright cornflower-blue eyes always

managed to captivate anyone within her orbit. "We're going to create the cutest hand-sewn journals and give them to everyone at the shower. Then they'll fill them with memories of the couple, poetry, marital inspirations, anything really, and on their wedding day I'll tie the books together with a satin bow, like they used to do with stacks of love letters in the old days, and we'll present them to Miranda and Jesse."

"How wonderful!" Kay said.

"These are really easy to make. The thicker, larger paper stock is for the cover." Vicki held up the ecru paper. "Go ahead and fold it in half. Take a stack of seven sheets of the smaller paper and fold them in half, then place them inside the cover."

"Why seven sheets and not ten?" Tess asked.

"The wedding's on the fourteenth and seven sheets folded in half gives the book fourteen pages."

"You've thought of everything, Vicki," Maggie praised. "Isn't she smart to come up with this idea?"

She probably read it in a magazine.

Tess's conscience gave her a swift jab, but she couldn't help it. Vicki loved her artsy projects, and when they'd built their house, Brandon made sure to include a craft room for his bride. The kind with shallow drawers to hold card stock and a set of rods for spools of ribbon and paper. Not to mention the sewing station complete with four different types of machines and the knitting cubbies everyone swore held more yarn than Stitch in Time, which was around the corner from the Magpie, did on its store shelves.

Tess could design multilevel, graphic websites for global corporations yet Vicki Homemaker still made her feel inadequate. Crafty, Tess wasn't. The one time she'd tried her hand at quilting, she'd almost asphyxiated herself on rubber cement.

"After what Miranda did for me at my baby shower," Vicki added, "I think I owe her one."

The women filled Tess in on the details she didn't already know about one of the biggest events to hit Ramblewood in years. The way they talked, Miranda was practically a superhero and Tess was dying to meet her. "Take the awl and punch a hole in the middle of the seam, then two more equally spaced on either side." Vicki demonstrated, pulling a piece of cork from her bag to place under the book. "Everyone take some cork so Kay doesn't murder us for ruining her counter. And then we'll stitch some waxed twine through the holes and we're done."

The women followed suit, telling Tess more Miranda tales. "I swear," Mable said, "that child has some sass, but underneath beats a heart of pure gold."

"Wouldn't it be wonderful if she and Jesse adopted Ever?" Maggie said. "They'd make great parents."

"I didn't know they were thinking about adopting Ever," Tess said. For some inexplicable reason the idea bothered her.

"I don't think the timing is right for them." Vicki added another finished journal to her stack while the others still plodded away on their first one. "Plus, that house isn't exactly suitable for Ever, especially with the number of stairs it has, and all the bedrooms are located on the second floor."

"Jesse told me they want to wait a few years before having kids," Kay added. "The house needs some serious renovating, all new plumbing, a new roof and probably new bathrooms when all is said and done. Jesse's trying to expand his business and they have their hands full right now."

"When the time comes, they'll make great parents," Maggie said.

"Anyone would be blessed to adopt Ever." Tess felt like her heart was on the verge of splitting in two at the thought of the little girl without a family to call her own. "I wish I could."

"You?" Maggie cackled. "That's the funniest thing I've heard this year. You're not even married."

Tess stared at her mother in disbelief. Looking around at the other women, she noticed that none of them had cracked a smile, unless you counted Vicki's *what's stopping you* brow raise.

"In all fairness, Maggie, you don't have to be married to have children," Mable said. "Many of the young folk today adopt children on their own."

"Oh, I don't know," Vicki added. "I thought you and Cole looked pretty friendly together last night, and he's wonderful with Randi Lynn. Any chance of rekindling that relationship?"

"We're just learning to be friends again," Tess said. She looked at her mother, who stood at the end of the counter, shaking her head and laughing to herself. "Gee, Mom, thanks for the support."

"I think you'd be a great mother." Kay reached over the island and patted Tess's hand before shooting Maggie a stern look.

"Oh, come now." Maggie wiped her eyes. "Honey, I don't mean to offend you, but let's face it. You've never once expressed wanting kids. Some people aren't cut out to have children. You're too—"

"Too what, mother?" Tess dared.

"Taking care of a child with cerebral palsy is no

small thing. Where is all this coming from?" Maggie looked truly puzzled.

"Just because I haven't vocalized wanting children doesn't mean I don't want them."

Tess hadn't ruled out children. In fact, she hadn't given the matter much thought until she started dating Cole a few years ago. After they broke up, Tess's career took precedence over almost everything once again, and she unfailingly followed the goals she'd set for herself when she graduated college.

But things had dramatically changed in her life now, and she felt ready to consider adoption.

"Who do you even know in New York that has children?" Maggie asked. "Your phone calls are like listening to reruns of *Sex and the City*. You're too into yourself and your career."

"I think you should go for it," Vicki chimed in from across the island. "At the very least, look into what's involved. Inquiring won't hurt anything and it's not like you have to make a commitment right away."

Encouraged by her friend, Tess gathered her things. "If you'll excuse me," she said, sliding her laptop into her bag. "I have some work to do."

"Where are you going?" Maggie called out behind her.

"Thanks for the support, everyone," Tess called over her shoulder, ignoring her mother's question.

THE MORNING SUN glimmered off the metal roof of the stables. It was the last project his father completed before his death. Joe didn't only supervise, he was on top of the barn with the rest of the crew, working right beside them.

Cole sat astride Blackjack, surveying the pasture of

yearlings. His father wanted his sons to take an active part in the ranch, and even though Shane, Chase and Cole wanted to ride the rodeo circuit, Joe couldn't have been prouder. There was always an understanding that after they'd had their fun and games, they would return to Bridle Dance and build their homes on this land.

Everyone except Jesse, that is. Jesse had returned to work on Bridle Dance after their father passed. But once he asked Miranda to marry him, it was obvious he belonged at Double Trouble, where they could create a legacy of their own.

Shane and Chase were still out riding the circuit, leaving the bulk of running Bridle Dance to Cole. Sure his brothers pulled their weight when they were around, but they weren't at the ranch day in and day out like he was and they didn't fully understand what it took to run the place. And that was precisely why Shane's bid for a rodeo school irked Cole to no end.

As a Langtry, they were bound to honor those who rode the land before them, and Joe's wishes were to have a hippotherapy facility. The vision was to provide not only therapy to those who needed it, but a place for their families to stay, if they couldn't afford to go anywhere else.

Kay had welcomed the idea from the very beginning. Through the Langtrys' endowment at the regional hospital, they'd witnessed the struggles many of the families endured when they couldn't afford the equine therapy their loved ones required.

Smaller therapy ranches offered programs designed only for children and veterans but Joe saw the need for a grander facility and had already begun the process of interviewing the top therapists in the field.

Since his death, life and laughter on the ranch were

just what the doctor ordered, especially for their mother. Jesse and Cole had decided to call the facility Dance of Hope, combining part of the ranch's name and honoring their great-grandmother, Hope, the first matriarch of Bridle Dance. Kay loved the idea and immediately started on designs to renovate some of the old unused bunkhouses. The three of them had a plan and everyone was on board, or so they thought, until Shane strode into the family's great room one night and announced he wouldn't be going along with their father's dream anymore. He acknowledged the benefit of equine therapy, but said creating their own program was a money pit and hindered the ranch's future expansion.

Charity began at home, and he demanded the money be used for something profitable, like a rodeo school. Chase immediately followed suit once Shane brought everyone up to speed on the cost of running a hippotherapy operation.

But Cole knew Kay had never given up their father's dream. She kept it forefront in conversations with her children, with the underlying expectation that they would eventually come to an agreement. It broke Cole's heart to watch his mother pray for the best every day, only to go to bed no closer to a resolution.

He admired her devotion to her husband, even in his death. It was a love he thought he'd found with Tess and one he was sure he'd lost forever when she walked away. He knew kissing her again would be a mistake, but he'd wanted to see if there was anything left between them. Deny it all she wanted, Cole felt the passion they'd once shared. It was still there and he wasn't going to let it slip away that easily again.

"Those are some mighty big clouds you've got your head in." Nicolino Travisonno, their ranch foreman, walked his mount from the stable's side entrance, snapping Cole back to reality. "You and your brothers still battling?"

Nicolino had emigrated from Italy over twenty years ago and had been a ranch hand for Cole's father for almost as long. Growing up in the traditions of the *butteri,* as Italian cowboys were known, he opted not to wear chaps, preferring heavy cotton pants and a wide-brimmed hat from his native Tuscania. He even carried the traditional *mazzarella* staff Italian cowboys used to herd cattle and horses.

The foreman had taught Cole and his brothers to speak fluent Italian, which always impressed the women in their lives, although he doubted any of them could read or write a single word of the language. In turn, they'd introduced him to their cousin Ella Slater, and after fifteen years of marriage and five children, Nicolino was one of the family.

"I'm hoping we won't be much longer." Cole dismounted. "I think Tess might be able to convince Chase to see things our way."

"Ah, the torch has been relit, my friend." Nicolino placed his hand over his heart. "To the love that never should have ended in the first place."

"Do you mind convincing Tess of that?" Cole looked toward her car. "I've made a lot of mistakes when it comes to women."

"Only because you've been searching for her replacement all your life instead of chasing after the real thing."

"Okay, Obi-Wan." Cole laughed. "Enlighten me on how you arrived at this one."

"You pined for her all through school and never had the *coglioni* to do anything about it."

"You leave my *coglioni* out of this," Cole said. "I'll

admit I wanted to ask her out, but I didn't want to ruin the friendship if it didn't work out."

"Don't hand me that line of horseshit." Nicolino rolled his eyes. "You weren't smart enough back then to know anything about ruining a friendship. You bedded every girl you met trying to find someone like Tess. Then when the two of you broke up, you did it to forget her and you've continued to do it. She was your first love and has remained your only love, and until you admit it, you'll never find peace."

Cole stared at Nicolino. He couldn't argue with the man because he was right, and he also knew he'd make it work this time if Tess would give him one more chance.

"You said Tess might convince Chase to change his mind?" Nicolino asked. "Where will that leave Shane if she does?"

Cole hadn't given thought to the repercussions of everyone voting against his brother. The way Shane was acting lately, Cole didn't much care how he reacted. Shane had made his bed, and what he did in it was his problem. "He doesn't give a rat's tail how we feel, and believe me, that feeling will be reciprocated."

Shrugging off the thought of hurting Shane, Cole led Blackjack inside what their father famously called the horse mansion, given that the square footage was more than triple the size of the main house. Cole loosened the cinch on the horse's saddle, removed it and placed it on the middle branch of the wall-mounted saddle stand. A stableman walked over and led the horse to one of the ten grooming stalls that lined the far wall.

Back outside the stables, Nicolino swung into his saddle, looking down at Cole in the shadows of the inlayed stone archway.

"Just prepare yourself for fallout if it comes down to the entire family against Shane," Nicolino said. "He has a wild streak you may not be able to tame this time."

"One I'm not sure even I can tame," Jon Reese added, walking up the dirt path. "We need to prepare for the fight of your life, Cole."

Having his old friend back in town and on his side was a blessing Cole hadn't counted on. Not only did Jon have a history with the Langtrys, he'd been Miranda's best friend when she lived in Washington, D.C. He was also the one responsible for luring Miranda to town and convincing her to buy Double Trouble out from under Jesse to force him back home. Jon was definitely accustomed to all facets of the Langtry way of life.

"Someone's in a hurry." Nicolino nodded in the direction of the main house.

Tess bounded down the front steps, leaving her mother to stand in the doorway and watch. A few minutes later her rental car barreled along the road away from the ranch, leaving clouds of dust in her wake.

"Wager to guess what's got her so hotheaded today?" Jon eyed Cole suspiciously.

"Don't look at me," Cole said. "I ruffled her feathers at sunrise and it's well past noon now. Someone else will have to take the blame for this one."

Silently Cole wondered to himself what had riled Tess up so much she'd fled the bridal shower preparations. No one could deny she was spirited, but barreling out of his family's house was out of character. He'd love to go after her, but work demanded his complete focus and he cursed under his breath for constantly having to remind himself of that.

"You need to halt production on Dance of Hope until I can get everything resolved legally."

"What are you talking about?" Cole spun toward his friend. "I'm paying you to overthrow my brother and you come here and tell me he wins?"

"Shane's not winning anything." Jon placed a hand on Cole's shoulder for reassurance. "But he can and will shut you down if you continue to move forward. You're using Bridle Dance to bankroll this expansion and you can't do that without majority vote. You knew this from day one, yet you and Kay kept moving ahead. I heard from Jesse you've added Tess to the payroll and you know you can't do that, Cole."

"I didn't," Cole said. "My mother did."

"Kay can't hire anyone when it comes to the business," Jon said. "This does not belong to your mother anymore. It belongs to you and your brothers, leaving her control over the land and the house, not the ranch. Certainly she understands that."

"Of course she does, but she also wants to finish what my father started. Believe me, I didn't want Tess here," Cole growled. "But she's already done more in a couple days than we expected her to do in a few weeks. I'm not firing Tess. I need her!"

Jon drew back at Cole's declaration, covering his face with the palms of his hands and running them across his stubble of a beard.

"I didn't mean it that way," Cole stammered. "I meant—"

"You have to leave your personal feelings for Tess out of this." Jon lowered his voice so none of the grooms would overhear any more of their conversation. "If you keep her on the payroll it better be under the guise of some legitimate Bridle Dance employment, not Dance of Hope. The more stunts you pull, the more likely a judge will decide in Shane's favor."

Cole hated to admit Jon was right. His personal feelings were clouding his judgment where the ranch was concerned. Not only with Tess, but with his mother, too. Both were strong, take-charge women, and unfortunately he'd let them both run with this project. "I don't want to meet here anymore so you'll have to come to my office next time." Jon stepped into his new, fully loaded, metallic-red BMW Z4 convertible roadster, purchased no doubt with his father's money from their little arrangement earlier this year. "Too many ears around, and who knows how many have been bribed by Shane for information."

Cole hadn't considered his brother might pay their employees on the side to spy for him. But Jon knew his way around bribes and payoffs after Joe hired him to drive Jesse home to Bridle Dance. Everything was forgiven after Joe died and those involved realized there wasn't any malice involved, simply a father wanting his family together. But Cole couldn't help wondering if those same people Jon and his father paid off were now working with Shane.

Cole hated suspecting everyone around him to be a traitor. When had his life turned into such a soap opera? Remembering his promise to Tess, he called Eileen at Monkey Junction to find out when Ever's next session was.

Then, before he could change his mind, Cole punched Tess's number into his phone. He'd ask her out to dinner later and tell her the good news. And at the same time he'd satisfy his burning curiosity and find out who or what had caused her flight from the ranch.

Chapter Six

Tess strode out of the Ramblewood Public Library, her arms filled with books on adoption and cerebral palsy. She wanted the facts and she didn't trust everything she read online. What she didn't appreciate was paying the hundred-dollar nonresident library card fee. It wasn't like she was a stranger to town.

Fumbling with the door-lock button on the key fob, Tess noticed Chase Langtry walking into the Feed & Grain across the street. Tess tossed the books in the backseat of the car and quickly checked her reflection in the mirror. After a lip gloss touch-up, she ran across Shelby Street toward the store entrance.

Immediately she regretted the lip gloss—grain dust from the mill elevator flew everywhere. Swiping at her mouth, she climbed the stairs to the loading bay and casually scanned the vast store, trying to spot Chase among the rows of calf-milk replacer and cans of Bag Balm for sensitive udders. She turned the corner and found herself inches from the cowboy's chest.

"Lost?" Chase asked, leaning against the shelving unit and hooking his thumb over one of his championship belt buckles. "Last I checked the Daltons weren't raising dairy cows."

Tess gave a nervous laugh, which echoed in the open-raftered building. "Birdseed."

Great save! Tess thought to herself. "Mom sent me here to get birdseed and I have no idea where to find it." She grabbed a tin of Bag Balm from the shelf. "This stuff's great on dry hands. I'm buying some to take back to New York. Rough winters and all."

Chase frowned. "Birdseed, huh? Maggie couldn't pick up one of the small bags at the grocery store. She sent you over here for a hundred-pound bag of seed?"

All right, he had a point. "It's for the wedding. We're going to fill little bags of birdseed for the guests to throw at the end of the ceremony. Environmentally conscious, that sort of thing."

"Honey, what are you up to?" Chase drawled. "Even if every resident of Ramblewood was invited to the wedding you couldn't use that much birdseed."

"And suet balls," Tess rambled, trying to find a way to interject Dance of Hope into the conversation. "Mom's making suet balls for the birds this winter."

"Okay, you win. If it's birdseed you want, it's birdseed I'll help you find."

Tess flipped through the virtual yellow pages in her head and tried to think of a place she could order small satin bags to hold said birdseed. She prayed Vicki hadn't already thought of the idea, or she would spend the next ten years making suet balls for the entire county.

Chase hoisted a bag of seed over his shoulder as if it were nothing and strode to the counter. "Burrell, add this to my bill and the Bag Balm she's holding, too."

"Chase, what are you doing?" Tess fumbled for her wallet, realizing she'd left her bag in the car. "Crap, I have to run and grab my purse."

Both men regarded her for a moment. "Do you want

me to have it delivered with the rest of the grain you ordered?" Burrell Wentworth asked.

"No, I've got it." Chase sauntered to the automatic double doors, turned and waited for Tess to join him. "Where's your car?"

Tess looked across the street. "It's over there in the library parking lot."

Chase lowered the bag of seed to the ground. "You came to the Feed & Grain to buy an enormous bag of birdseed, but you parked your car at the library?"

Tess knew she was burying herself deeper and deeper by the moment and needed a temporary break so she could gather her thoughts.

"I was at the library when I remembered the seed." She pulled the key out of her pocket and started across the lot. "I'll be right back."

Tess sprinted across the street, and slammed the car door behind her as she slid beneath the wheel. Wiping away the remnants of her grain-dappled lip gloss, she jammed the key into the ignition and pulled out of one parking lot and into the next. Popping the trunk release, she hopped out and handed Chase the cash.

"Don't worry about it." Chase loaded the seed bag into her trunk. "After the five-thousand-some-odd-dollar order I just placed, what's a little birdseed? Buy me a drink some night at Slater's."

Sensing her opening, Tess jumped right in. "Tonight works for me so why don't you join me for dinner, my treat? My mouth started watering for the Ragin Cajun the instant my plane landed."

"Ragin Cajun?" Chase contemplated her invite. "Happens to be my favorite place to eat. Okay, I'll bite, so to speak, because I'm dying to see how this plays out."

"There is nothing playing out, Chase," Tess reassured. "I'm repaying the favor, that's it, no games. How does six sound?"

"I'll meet you there."

THE RAGIN CAJUN stood two doors down from Slater's Mill, overlooking Cooter Creek. They dined out on the brightly painted enclosed porch, enjoying the zydeco music. The place was lively and had an invigorating vibe you felt down to your toes.

"Out of all my travels, I still haven't been to New Orleans," Chase said, sucking on a boiled crawfish. "Every time I come here, I promise myself I'll make it to one of the rodeo events, but I never do."

"So promise me, instead," Tess said, over her shrimp étouffée. "Then you'll have to keep it. You wouldn't want to let me down, would you?'

"No, I wouldn't want to do that." Chase stared blankly at her then shook his head.

"When's the next rodeo there?"

"April," Chase said.

"Then April it is." Tess pulled her iPhone from her bag, punching NOLA into the calendar. "You be sure to give me the exact dates and we'll go together. I'd love to show you around some of my favorite places. I've never found anyone willing to do the nighttime cemetery tour with me so I guess that means you're elected! It'll be fun."

"You're serious, aren't you?' Chase leaned back in his chair.

"Serious as the business end of a .45." Tess raised her lemon-drop martini. "To New Orleans in April."

"Why were you at the library today?" Chase asked, snapping her to the present. "Seems like a strange place to spend your vacation."

"I was doing some research," she said, uncertain how much she should tell him.

"On the Langtry brother feud, I presume." Chase clearly had no desire to discuss his family's issues.

"No actually, on something else." Tess let out a slow, deep breath. "I'm thinking about adopting Ever, and I wanted to know more about cerebral palsy," she confided.

Bracing herself for berating laughter, she was relieved to look up and see Chase mulling over her words. Sure, the Langtry men were a sexy lot, but Chase was a tad more reserved and shy than the other three. He didn't mock or tease her. And the fact he took her seriously gave her the confidence she needed to see things through.

"It's a big responsibility," he said. "Are you sure you're ready to tackle being a single parent?"

A smile spread across her face, and she leaned over to give Chase a quick kiss.

"What's that for?" he asked.

"For not mentioning the whole special-needs thing."

"You're an intelligent woman." Chase covered her hand with his as she sat back down. "I assumed you already factored that part into the equation."

"It's only preliminary research, and I can't help think what a rewarding challenge it would be. Tim never wanted children. My career didn't allow me much time to consider the possibilities of having kids, but my life is different now. I really feel I can give Ever a good home and the mother she deserves."

She slid her chair next to Chase's and proceeded to share what she'd learned over the past couple days. He listened intently, offering his two cents every now and then.

"My brother's never gotten over you," Chase said after they ordered another round of drinks.

"Somehow I find that hard to believe." Tess chortled, trying to push last night out of her mind. "I've heard stories involving his little conquests since we broke up. My God, he's even listed in a buckle bunny internet forum as 'good in bed but don't expect him to buy you breakfast in the morning.' We were childhood friends that took a stab at something more and failed. It happens. It wasn't a love story, there was no happy ending—it was, and then it wasn't."

"Cole was going to propose to you in Vegas."

For a moment, Tess wondered if he had planned to make the declaration or if it merely fell out of his mouth. Not exactly wanting to hear more yet afraid not to, she said, "Wh-why are you telling me this?" She placed her hand on her chest and was surprised at how warm she felt. She didn't know if it was the last lemon martini or the idea of Cole asking her to marry him.

"Because you walked out on the most important night of your life and it's time you knew the truth."

Chase detailed every moment of the proposal Cole had painstakingly planned for Tess. Not knowing whether to cry or scream, she opted to remain silent and listen. There was no way she could have known Cole would have gone to such great lengths, even prebooking their wedding date. But romantic as it sounded, she knew he would never be happy living anywhere but Ramblewood. It was an impossible situation, yet one she'd desperately wanted.

She missed the times they'd spent together. Their walks along the streets of all the rodeo towns where he'd competed. Their annual attempt at skating in Rockefeller Center, which usually meant both of them sitting on the ice laughing at each other. She missed Cole's friendship, and their long kisses goodbye, but she loved the anticipation of their next visit.

Tess shook her head to erase the images. Marriage would never have worked and Tess refused to feel guilty over something that didn't happen. She'd done them both a favor by walking away. He'd bedded the first half of the county phone book before they'd started dating, and from what she'd heard since they'd split, he was making his way through the second half. No, she wouldn't give it another thought—until she became aware that Cole was standing at the side of their table.

Chase tried to stand up so fast he would have taken his chair with him if Tess hadn't kept a firm grip on his biceps.

"Hey, Cole, this isn't—"

"Wh-what brings you here?" Tess stammered, her voice escaping her. She met Cole's eyes and tried to envision him proposing to her. Would he get down on one knee? Or would he hide the ring in her dessert?

"I saw your car outside, figured you were dining alone, so I thought I'd join you." Cole stood firmly in place, not making eye contact with his brother. "My mistake."

"There's always room for one more." Tess motioned to a nearby chair with her free hand, keeping her death grip on Chase with the other. Why was Cole practically glaring at them when he was the one who'd asked her to talk to Chase? "I'm sure you can squeeze in."

"No, thanks." Cole glanced down. "I've been trying to reach you for a few hours."

"I was at the library earlier." Tess pulled her phone from her pocket and slid the ringer switch back on, noticing the sixteen missed calls and eight text messages. Curious to know if they were all from him, she placed the phone back in her bag without looking. "I must have forgotten to turn the volume up again. Is everything all right?"

"I called Monkey Junction and Ever will be there tomorrow morning at nine." Cole shifted awkwardly, and then met her gaze, instantly unsettling her. "I won't be able to go, but maybe Chase can tag along for the ride."

"Why do I suddenly feel ambushed?" Chase said under his breath. "You two planned this, didn't you?"

Tess didn't want Chase to think she'd set him up and shot Cole a pleading glance. That may have been the plan in the beginning, but once she and Chase started talking, the thought didn't cross her mind again. Both brothers looked hurt, making Tess feel like the guiltiest woman on the planet.

"I'm entirely capable of driving myself up there, Cole. I don't need a chaperone." Tess wanted to make Chase understand this wasn't a setup, but Cole seemed determined to push the matter further and continue with his plan. But why did he look so wounded?

"Since we're her benefactors, a Langtry should be present—"

"Stop it, will you," Chase interrupted. "I have no problem being one of Ever's benefactors, Cole, and you know it. And you also know that doesn't mean we have to be there each time she is. We pay her expenses, nothing else, so stop trying to guilt me into seeing her."

"Shane really has his hooks in you, doesn't he?" Cole snorted.

"Guys, please," Tess begged, looking around the restaurant. "People are beginning to stare."

Ignoring her, Chase rose, matching his brother in height. "It won't make the ranch any money, Cole. I'm not changing my vote." He turned to face Tess. "And I don't appreciate being used, either."

Chase headed for the door.

"You wanted me to convince him to see things your way," Tess said, rising from her chair. "We were having a nice friendly conversation. Nothing more, so why do you look like I broke just your heart?"

Not wanting to hear his answer, Tess hurried off to follow Chase. But as she did, she could have sworn Cole muttered under his breath, "Too late for that."

AT THE FRONT entrance to the Ragin Cajun, Cole watched Tess try to convince his brother not to leave. He'd told Tess to go after Chase, practically guilted her into it, but he was unprepared for the emotions that came along with actually seeing her cozied up to him in a restaurant.

The last time he'd seen Tess with another man was in high school. Fiercely academic, she managed to have her share of boyfriends in between riding competitions and the debate club. Annoyed at himself for letting it get to him, Cole exited through the side door of the restaurant.

Standing by the bank of Cooter Creek, Cole remembered the night he'd escorted Tess to prom after her date bailed on her for the rodeo, instead. He thought he could finally work up the nerve to ask her out during their last dance, but fear of rejection and losing his best friend if she turned him down made him chicken out. Once he took the chance ten years later, it was one hell of a ride.

He thought he'd moved past Las Vegas, and Nicolino was right—he did try to convince himself he was over Tess with every woman he took to bed. None of them compared to Tess, not that he would know what bedding her was like since he vowed to make their first time more than an abbreviated weekend together. He'd loved Tess and wanted everything to be flawless.

Christmas was the unspoken plan since they were both heading home for the holidays after the National Finals Rodeo. But Cole thought the night he proposed would to be their first *night* together since he'd planned to escort Tess home to New York and stay with her until they left for Texas. Only, that night never came.

Telling Tess he was fine with her flirting with Chase was a stupid move on his part, but right now he was more annoyed at his brother for going along with it. Their father had scheduled them to break ground on Dance of Hope's indoor arena the first of October. They were long overdue and the contractors had made it clear they were no longer able to wait for the Langtrys to come to an agreement. Every day that passed cost money and Cole was unable to pay them for their time since the finances were contingent on a majority vote. Tess working on Chase was his last hope and one he now hated he'd set in motion.

Cole walked along the creek path to Slater's Mill, hoping to lose himself among friends for an hour or two. From the water's edge, Cole spotted Shane on the back porch of the honky-tonk, cozying up to one of Ramblewood's former cheerleaders, now a single mother of three.

"Do you want to be called for breakfast or should I just blow in your ear?" Cole heard his brother say. Leave it to Shane to pick a woman with baggage.

Not wanting to risk a run-in with another brother, Cole drifted back down the creek walk to his truck.

"What was that about?" Tess demanded, stepping out from the shadows. "You told me to invite him to dinner and then you barreled in like a jealous boyfriend."

The moon highlighted her features, removing any trace of anger she may have felt for him. Not wanting to miss another opportunity, he closed the distance between them and took her face between his hands.

"No more games, Tess," he whispered against her mouth, gently kissing her lips until they parted for him. "I was wrong in asking you to get involved. The last thing I want is to see you with another man."

"Is that so?" Tess questioned coyly.

"Tell me you still feel something between us," Cole said. "Tell me it's not too late."

"I do, Cole, but I don't know where this is going."

"Where do you want it to go?" Not waiting for an answer, Cole dipped his head for another taste.

Traces of lemon lingered on her tongue, causing him to tug her closer, allowing him to taste her depths further. Hearing voices behind them, Cole maneuvered Tess against the oak tree beyond the Still 'N' Grill's back entrance. Hidden from view, he slipped one hand under the edge of her scarlet, gauzy chemise, raising gooseflesh along her skin. Tess shivered, drawing herself closer to him while she threaded her hands behind his neck. She tasted him, one leg sliding up his outer thigh, her cowboy-booted foot wrapping around his waist. His own arousal grew, and leaning back slightly, he pressed himself fully against her.

"Show me what Vegas would have been like that night if things had gone differently," she purred.

Cole let out a deep groan, and, unable to control himself any longer, he dragged himself out of her embrace and quickly led her by the hand to his truck. Grabbing the side of the truck bed, she kept her back to him. His arms wrapped around her waist, making their way underneath her shirt until he cupped her breasts. Tess reached under her shirt, and in an instant, her breasts were free and bare.

"Gotta love a front-hook bra," Cole growled against her neck.

Tess tilted her head until it rested on his shoulder. "Do you want me, Cole?"

Cole reached for the door handle of the cab and swung it open. His head swam at the reality that the moment he'd waited for half his life was about to come true. Never had he wanted someone more than he wanted Tess. He knew she still had a piece of his heart, a bigger piece than he'd been willing to admit until now.

"More than you know."

Spinning her around, Cole lifted her up onto the seat. At eye level, her shirt still raised, breasts exposed to him, he leaned in, tasting one hardened nipple. Tess tilted back, flicking the overhead light off.

"Show me," Tess whispered.

Engulfed in darkness, Cole climbed in the truck after her, while she removed her jacket and the rest of her top. Reaching for his jeans, she unzipped them, urging them past his hips. After a slight hesitation on his part, he allowed himself to drop every wall he'd built around his heart, and during the course of the next few hours, the windows steamed and cleared numerous times. Thankfully, the Ragin Cajun parking lot was full when he'd pulled in, forcing him to park in the deserted Creek Tours & Tackle lot next door.

This was not how Cole had envisioned their first night together. The front of a pickup was a long way from a luxurious suite at the Stratosphere overlooking Las Vegas, but it was their night. His body ached from the contorted positions dictated by the bench seat. Looking over, he saw Tess fastening her bra. He reached for her to stop and tried to pull her closer, only to be swatted away.

"Cole, I have to get home," Tess said matter-of-factly. "My parents will be worried, it's late."

"Your parents probably think you're at the ranch, and we've been out plenty later than this, Tess. It's not even ten o'clock."

Tess quickly dressed, leaving Cole with a sudden coldness. He reached again for her to stop, but she yanked her arm away. He jerked on his own clothes and they sat in silence for the next few minutes.

"You know I'm headed home to New York after the wedding, right?" Tess asked.

"That was the original plan, but what about the website and the marketing you're going to work on with my mother?"

At this point Cole didn't care that he was supposed to stop her from working on the project. He wanted to keep her as close to him as possible.

"What I don't finish here, I can do at home until you find someone permanent to fill the position. We both knew *this* was temporary, right?"

Tess's words hung heavy in the air while she fumbled for her keys. Usually Cole was the one who couldn't wait to get dressed and head out, and all he wanted to do was hold her until the sun came up.

"Not if you stay here." He bit back the words *with me* when he saw her hand resting on the door handle.

"I've already sent out my résumé to quite a few places and I contacted a headhunter before I left. My home is in New York, where I have an established career."

"No, Tess, you have a profession. One you can do anywhere in the world if you chose. And presently you're out of work with no place to go. Why else would you be here? Who are you trying to convince, you or me?"

"I'm here for your brother's wedding, Cole. You know that. I'll have another job soon enough, but I also wanted to spend some time with my family."

"Come on, this is me you're talking to. Since you didn't come home for the funeral, believe me, no one would have thought twice if you'd missed the wedding. You're here for one reason and one reason alone. You're feeling a little lost and you needed to ground yourself and figure out what's next. I know you better than anyone else does. Ramblewood is where you belong and deep in your heart you know it, too. You wouldn't be so interested in seeing Ever again if you planned on running back to New York. The Tess I know would never get that close to a child just to leave."

Tess didn't respond. Instead, the door spring creaked when she opened it, her feet clacking against the ground when she jumped down. Cole leaped out of the truck to follow her.

"At least let me walk you to your car."

Tess didn't stop for him to catch up with her. Crossing the adjacent lots, he remained a few feet behind her, making sure she was safely inside her car before he tramped back to the truck.

"Dammit!" He smacked the fender of the pickup. "How did I let her get under my skin again?"

Annoyed at himself for letting his guard down, he clambered into the cab, immediately welcomed by the scent of her perfume. Starting the engine, he lowered the windows, inviting in the crisp evening air for the drive home. So they had sex. Years in the making, it was finally over and done with and now he could get her out of his system for good.

The house was unusually dark when he drove up and parked. Outside of his mother's Mercedes, no other cars were in sight. For the past month, Cole couldn't remember a night when someone involved in the wedding or one of the church ladies wasn't over.

"Mom," Cole called out, entering the mudroom. "Mom, are you home?"

He placed his hat on the hat rack and slid his boots off using the bootjack his father built into the floor when they were kids. Placing them to the side, he stepped into the darkened kitchen. After he searched the entire first and second floors of the house, with no sign of his mother, he figured she must be out with a friend. He grabbed a beer from the fridge, flopped down on one of the leather couches in the great room and turned on the television.

From where he sat, he noticed the cellar door was open a crack, light barely visible. Setting his beer on the table, Cole padded down the stairs into the expansive finished basement. His mother had her own separate wing, containing her sewing and gift-wrapping rooms. His father had his darkroom and library, and the stone-encased wine cellar sat at the far corner of the house. His father loved dramatic rooms, and the cellar didn't fail to disappoint. But it paled in comparison with the one he'd built underneath the winery.

Cole heard a hint of a sound coming from the library and slowly pushed the door open. His mother sat curled up on one of the Italian leather wing chairs, holding one his father's many journals.

"Mom, are you all right?" Cole asked cautiously.

Looking up from the book, she placed the red ribbon

marker between the pages and closed the cover. Removing her glasses, she set them next to a rocks glass he assumed contained cognac, his mother's drink of choice.

"I'm fine, honey." Kay looked at her watch and rubbed the back of her neck. "You're home early."

"One of those nights." Cole didn't offer any further explanation and Kay didn't press. "No wedding festivities tonight?"

"I love your brother dearly," Kay said. "But how much wedding stuff can one person take? And to think I have to go through this with all of you boys?"

"Well, I don't think you have to worry about me anytime soon," Cole reassured. "And didn't you volunteer to plan this wedding for Miranda?"

"Because she didn't have any family to do it for her." Kay stood, placing the journal on the shelf among the other volumes. "If I offer to do something this crazy again, please have me committed."

Dark circles shadowed his mother's eyes, proving once again that she hadn't slept the night before.

"I remember when you boys would run wild throughout this house," Kay said, leading the way out of the cellar. "Now you fight with each other nonstop."

Knowing he had to tell her what Jonathan said earlier about ceasing all work on Dance of Hope until they were legally cleared to do so, he took a swig of his beer from the coffee table and refilled his mother's cognac glass.

"Mom, I need to talk to you," Cole said, angling them toward the chess table next to the two-story glass window overlooking the ranch.

"What happened?" Kay grabbed the glass from his hand and took a sip before she sat down. "Okay, kiddo, lay it on me."

"We have to stop working on Dance of Hope until Jon gives us the go-ahead. If we don't—"

"Horsefeathers!" Kay rose and started to walk away with a wave of her hand. "I will do no such thing."

"It's not your money, Mom," Cole called out after her. "It's Bridle Dance's and I'm sorry, but you have no right to spend it how you see fit."

"I raised the four of you single-handedly while your father worked himself to death on this ranch. I've put more blood and tears into this place than all of you boys combined and you tell me I don't have a say in any of it."

"Not the business end." Cole's voice lowered. "Shane is going to legally shut us down if we continue to use any more of the ranch's finances to fund this project. And that includes Tess."

"I have never felt more like a stranger in my own life than I do this very moment." Kay sat on the edge of the couch and placed her glass on the slate table. "I'll pay for it myself."

"What?" Cole didn't fathom his mother's meaning at first. "Mom, we're talking millions of dollars."

"I didn't want it to come to this, but if my accounts run dry and it means selling the land you boys happen to lease from me, then so be it." Kay rose defiantly in front of her eldest son. "One way or another, Dance of Hope is happening whether anyone likes it or not. No one is going to tell me what I can't do on my land. Do I make myself clear?"

"Yes, ma'am." Cole stood as his mother left the room. Tossing back the remains of the cognac he'd poured for her, he laughed. "I'll be damned, Mom, you've still got it."

Chapter Seven

Five-in-the morning phone calls were never a good thing, especially from a number she didn't recognize.

"Hello," Tess grumbled. She had fully intended on getting at least three hours' sleep before she drove to Monkey Junction.

Ricky jumped up on the bed, nudging the phone from her hand and purring so loudly she couldn't hear the voice on the other end of the line. Sitting up, Tess cradled the feline in her lap, rubbing his mostly white tummy.

"Tess, can you hear me?" a man called out from the phone.

"Who is this?" Tess asked. "And why are you calling me so early?"

"It's Chase. I'm sorry if I woke you, I thought you were an early riser."

"Chase?" Tess rubbed her eyes, causing Ricky to reach up with his paw and try to bring her hand toward him for more morning affections. "Normally I am, but I decided to sleep in."

"Do you have a minute?"

"I guess, now that you got my attention." Tess reached for the old-fashioned dual-bell alarm clock next to the bed and mentally ticked off the time she needed to drive to Monkey Junction. "Did you change your mind about coming with me, because we don't have to leave this early."

"I haven't changed my mind." His voice sounded solemn. "You haven't told my brother what I told you about the proposal, have you?"

"No—"

"Please don't, Tess. I thought you should know, but please don't say anything to him, at least not right now. He'll probably tell you himself now that you're back in town, but let it come from him. He'll kill me if he finds out and that will cause more problems."

"I wouldn't even know how to bring the subject up." Tess yawned. "Excuse me. Your secret's safe with me."

"And I wanted to apologize for the way I acted last night. I know my brother put you up to that."

"He asked me to try to change your mind about the therapy facility," Tess agreed. "But that's as far as it went. I really enjoyed spending time with you and I appreciate you hearing me out where Ever is concerned. That was genuine, Chase. Please realize that. You're super easy to talk to and I'd actually like to do it again."

"Honey, don't get me wrong," he began. "Any man on this earth would be lucky to be on the receiving end of your affections. But you've had a firm grip on my brother's heart since the day you were born and I'm not going to go messing around that briar patch."

"Eww, I didn't mean it that way! What the heck is wrong with you Langtry men? And for the record, Cole and I had a two-month relationship a couple of years ago." Tess couldn't believe she was getting the *can we be friends* speech this early in the morning. "But I do think you and Bridgett should go out some night."

"Nah, I asked her out once and she told me I wasn't her type."

"Maybe you should try again." Tess knew Bridgett was picky when it came to men, but if a hot cowboy worth a fortune wasn't her type, Tess needed to have a talk with that girl.

"And maybe you should focus on your own love life instead of mine." Chase laughed. "I just wanted to say I was sorry for ruining dinner last night. Drive safely today."

"Will do," Tess said, before hanging up the phone.

She rolled onto her side and pulled the covers up over her head. The memory of the feel of Cole's body against hers had kept her awake throughout the night, and even after her shower, his scent still lingered. She had never intended to have sex with him, let alone feel any sort of attachment afterward. She'd bolted from the truck before the words *I love you* fell from her lips. She knew it was cruel to leave like that, but she'd never expected to feel the way she had.

Hearing about Cole's proposal plans complicated her feelings further. Would he have really uprooted his life for her so they could be together? The rodeo and the ranch were his entire world, at least until his father died. Yet Tess had seen a lot of changes in Cole in the past week, particularly regarding his determination to start the Dance of Hope. Was he really ready for marriage— and did he really want to marry her?

Was Chase right? Did I make the biggest mistake of my life walking away?

By the time Tess made her way downstairs, her mother was gone and her father was showering. She grabbed a travel mug and poured a large coffee, leaving a note on the counter saying she'd be out for a while but offering no further explanation. After her mother's reaction at Bridle Dance yesterday, Maggie was the last person she wanted to confide in.

As she drove toward Main Street, she cast a quick glance in the direction of the Magpie, but saw no sign of her mother. Once out of town, the ice-blue Focus zipped along the highway with ease and Tess found herself actually enjoying her economy cracker box of a car.

Singing along to vintage Skid Row, she turned up the volume in an attempt to drown out the memories of Cole that flooded her brain. Of course, a song like "I Remember You" didn't help matters any. Changing the station, she settled on a country station with fast, upbeat songs, which did the trick until the Faith Hill and Tim McGraw duet "It's Your Love" began to play.

"Are you kidding me?" Tess punched the scan button, listening to five-second clips of the stations, hoping one would suit her mood. Just when she was giving up, Joan Jett's "I Hate Myself for Loving You" screamed through the speakers. Tess stopped the scan, cranked the volume and belted along until her voice was hoarse.

After a thousand more station changes, Tess arrived at Monkey Junction. The place bustled in the morning hours. Everywhere people in shirts marked *Volunteer* across the back prepped the various areas for riders. A man Tess presumed was Bingo waved and rode by on a golf cart with Shorty beside him. Ominous clouds threatened to unleash their fury and Tess prayed the rain held off until after Ever's session. Entering into the empty front office, she read the various accreditations on the wall Cole had pointed out to her the other day.

Not unlike a doctor's office, each instructor and therapist had their PATH International certificates framed and proudly displayed. The American Hippotherapy

Association logo at the top of the wall led you down a pyramid of awards.

"Good morning, Tess." Eileen entered the office, looking over her shoulder. "Looks like a storm's brewing out there."

"You don't ride in the rain, do you?" Tess asked.

"We have a small enclosed area in case it does." Eileen tuned in to The Weather Channel on the television mounted in the far corner. "It's a rough enclosure, but it works in a pinch. The indoor arena Cole's planning for Dance of Hope has me envious already."

"Is Ever's therapist around? Her next appointment arrived before I was able to meet her and I'm interested in hearing how Ever's therapy works. I don't want to keep her from anything, but if she has a moment, I'd love to chat with her."

"Sure." Eileen stepped out onto the sidewalk. "Nancy, when you have a minute, would you mind coming in here?" Turning her attention to Tess, she added, "When Cole called I thought he'd be joining you."

"Last-minute change of plans." Tess fully expected to run into Cole when she pulled in the parking lot. Knowing how much Ever meant to him, she was surprised he would miss the opportunity to spend time with her. After one visit, the small precocious child had her rethinking her life completely. Vacations and promotions had less meaning since she'd met this wondrous tiny person with the sunny disposition. And in turn made Tess realize she needed a brighter disposition herself.

"Hello, it's nice to see you again." Nancy outstretched her hand. "I'm sorry we didn't have a chance to talk the other day."

"Tess, this is Nancy, our physical therapist extraordinaire," Eileen said, with a humorous bow. "Tess has some therapy questions." Eileen grabbed her slicker from the office closet and headed for the door. "I'll be back in a few."

"How long have you been a hippotherapist?" Tess asked the bubbly woman. Her short pixie cut accentuated her rosy cheeks and beaming smile. Everyone appeared happy at Monkey Junction.

"Actually, there's no such thing as a hippotherapist," Nancy said. "I'm a physical therapist specializing in hippotherapy, and my husband, Roger, who hasn't arrived yet, is an occupational therapist. A person's individual needs determine which of us they'll work with. But since everything here is pretty much a team dynamic, sometimes you'll have five of us involved in a session."

"And in Ever's situation?"

"Ever's progress was slow going at first, but over the past few months, her improvements have been remarkable. I credit her foster family for taking the time to research hippotherapy and for bringing her here."

"This type of therapy isn't the norm?" Tess wondered how something proven to change a person's quality of life wasn't a mandatory course of action.

"I wish it was," Nancy said. "It's considered holistic, and even in this day and age, it's still not fully accepted by many doctors."

"Will Ever continue to progress or will she remain at this level?"

"There's no certainty, but I'm working closely with her physician. I modify her program slightly each week by shifting her riding position or changing the horse's gait. The combination helps strengthen and stretch different parts of her body."

"Will she always require therapy?" Tess said, glancing out the window to see if the clouds had cleared any.

"Yes, but not necessarily this type. Ever has a list of exercises she does at home and she attends other physical therapy sessions. Hippotherapy's a big part of it, though. But when she gets older, she'll be able to carry out much of what she's learned on her own. Including hippotherapy, if she has access to horses. Therapy is the key to Ever's physical well-being. Her foster family has been wonderful with her, but hopefully she will find a place of her own."

Caitlin popped her head in the door. "I'm sorry to interrupt, but Miss Ever has arrived." Making a swooping motion with her arms, Caitlin grabbed a few plastic tiaras from behind the counter, placing one on her head and handing Nancy and Ever theirs. "Ever said she wanted to be a princess this Halloween, so I picked these up for everyone to wear."

"Halloween!" Tess completely forgot about the holiday. She quickly donned her crown, wishing she'd brought Ever some sort of treat.

"Don't worry." Caitlin tucked a few pieces of candy in Tess's hand. "We have you covered."

"Thank you." Tess ticked off a mental note to herself. *Be aware of children's holidays when becoming a parent.*

Outside, everyone wore a tiara, including some of the men. Bingo rolled out a runner to mimic a red carpet and Eileen stood waiting with a feather boa in her hands. Ever's foster mom slid the van door open and Ever cheered loudly.

Once out of the van, she made her bejeweled royal entrance. "CC's girlfriend is here." The pint-size princess had her jack-o'-lantern treat bucket attached to her wrist. "Where is CC?"

"He couldn't make it, sweetie." Tess hated the crest-

fallen look that suddenly appeared on the girl's face.
Plunking the candy Tess hid in her palm into the orange
pail, she asked, "But will I do?"

"Mmm." The little girl placed her finger over her
lips and looked skyward with squinted eyes. "I think
it will be okay."

Everyone around them laughed. Tess watched Lorraine slide the van door closed and climb back behind
the wheel. Tess called out to Ever's foster mom, but
Lorraine was already driving away.

Nancy had said Ever had a great foster family, but
why didn't Lorraine stick around during Ever's therapy
sessions? She wondered if the woman had other foster
children at home whom she had to attend to.

Nancy and Caitlin walked along either side of Ever
while she methodically placed one crutch in front of the
other with each step. They made their way to the first
corral where her horse waited, saddled and ready for
its rider. Caitlin fastened Ever's helmet and helped her
secure her vest. Her hands out wide, Ever waited for
someone to lift her into the saddle, smiling the entire
time. Once she was on the horse, she leaned forward
and hugged the animal's neck, giving him a quick kiss
before she started to ride.

"Yeah, Princess Ever!" Tess shouted.

"Come walk with me!" Ever yelled back.

Tess looked at Nancy and she nodded. "Sure, the
more the merrier."

Ever rode around the round pen, with Nancy and
Caitlin flanking either side. Tess noticed the knuckles
on Ever's hands were white from gripping the saddle
handles so tightly. The little girl focused her eyes on
the horse beneath her and nodded each time Nancy had
her shift slightly in the saddle.

"You're doing great, Ever," Nancy said. "The next

time you come we get to try another gait, but it's going to be a different horse, okay?"

"Can I still visit Poncho?"

"Of course, you can," Nancy reassured her. "Poncho's not going anywhere."

"Promise?" Ever asked.

Tess noticed a tear roll down the child's cheek and she tried to tilt her head to wipe it on her shoulder but she wasn't confident enough to let go of the saddle.

"What is it, sweetie?" Tess asked. "Why are you so upset?"

"I don't want Poncho to go away," Ever cried.

Tess choked back her own tears. For a child without a family to call her own, the animal probably meant more to her than it would to the other kids.

"No one is going to take Poncho away," Caitlin said. "In fact, we can have Poncho walk with us when you are on the other horse. Will that be all right?"

Ever nodded, smiling through her tears. After a few rumbles of thunder, they made their way into the covered area Eileen had mentioned earlier. The space was nothing more than an enlarged shed with bright fluorescent lights overhead. Unable to walk beside Ever, Tess flattened herself along the wall to prevent getting stepped on.

The plans she'd seen for Dance of Hope's enclosed arena included bleachers and pens containing staircases to allow riders to easily mount and dismount in a safe environment. Monkey Junction was a terrific facility, but she began to understand more of what Joe Langtry wanted to accomplish with his vision.

COLE WOKE WITH a heavy heart, knowing Ever would be disappointed he wasn't at Monkey Junction to see her this morning. While he wasn't present for every one of her sessions, he was there for a great deal of them, unless work interfered. He hoped Tess had managed to change Chase's mind last night before they left the restaurant. The thought hadn't occurred to him the rest of the evening, considering he'd been a little distracted.

Missing Ever's therapy today would be the one exception, he reasoned with himself, even though he really wanted to see her in the princess costume she'd been telling him about for the past month.

No matter how much he tried to shake Tess from his thoughts, she managed to invade them and his dreams. Now that he'd slept with her, he should be able to move on, but last night had had the opposite effect. The feel of her body against his seemed to have sent him into overdrive and he had to fight the desire to kidnap her from her family's house, take her away and make love to her for days on end. Cole jumped into an ice-cold shower to quell any further reckless ideas. Thoroughly chilled to the bone, he emerged and threw on some clothes.

The house was unusually quiet this morning. Shane most likely hadn't come home last night, thanks to his latest *Mill Girl* conquest, as they called the women who hung around Slater's looking for a little action. Padding barefoot past his parents' bedroom, he paused to listen at the door. Hearing nothing, he expected to find his mother down in the kitchen preparing a rancher's typical big breakfast, but was surprised to find it empty along with the rest of the house.

Stepping out on the back porch, Cole checked around the side of the house and saw her car was still there, but both of his brothers' trucks were gone. Concerned, he took the interior stairs two at a time until he reached the upper floor. Slowly opening Kay's bedroom door, he was relieved to see her sound asleep among the white down pillows and comforter.

Cole laughed to himself. "So that's what it took to get you to rest your fretful mind."

Staking claim on the land that was rightfully hers pretty much sealed the deal on Dance of Hope. That said, the implications of the plan would mean losing the business that was not only the family's bread and butter, but the legacy of four generations.

Cole didn't think things would come down to that. Shane may stand firm, but Chase would never allow the ranch to be torn asunder out of pure greed. Either way, they could build the facility and children like Ever would have a place to come to. But nothing would make Cole happier than Ever having a permanent place to call home.

Cole knew his chances for adopting Ever were slim. Even though agencies claimed not to discriminate based on sex, the fact Ever was young, female and had cerebral palsy placed her in a higher predator risk group.

The Langtrys would always provide for Ever, and then some. But Cole wanted to give her a stable and loving home and the ranch would be the ideal environment.

"Excuse me, sir," Billy Stevens, one of the grooms, called to him from the gate. "I'm sorry to bother you, but I think you need to look at Clover's front leg."

The mare had an infection from a cut she incurred on some downed fencing. Cole didn't trust many people to wrap a horse's leg. He'd witnessed too many horses rendered lame due to incorrect wraps, causing the tendon to bow.

Sliding on his boots, he followed Billy to the stables. The kid was a few months out of high school, graduating by the skin of his teeth, no thanks to his sorry excuse of a family. An abusive past had led him down the wrong road and he ended up doing a one-month stint in county lockup. When he got out he was scared straight and homeless, so the Langtrys gave him a chance and a place to live in one of the bunkhouses in exchange for working at the ranch. It wasn't much but it kept the kid off the streets and out of trouble. Cole tried talking Billy into going on to college, but his lack of self-esteem left him believing he'd never improve his situation.

Leaning over the stall door, Cole saw that Clover was very slightly favoring her left front leg. So slightly he might have missed it himself.

"Good call," Cole said. "Come with me."

Inside the medical supply room, Cole handed Billy a plastic tote. As he placed the items he needed inside, he explained the reasons for each. Unlatching the stable door, Cole stepped inside, motioning for Billy to follow.

"Easy girl." Billy instinctively ran his hand down the horse's shoulder and over her withers, remaining in her line of sight so not to spook her. "It's going to be all right."

Clover didn't mind Billy's presence, leading Cole to believe the young man had developed a trust level with the horses.

"Step around here, so you can see what I'm doing." Cole removed the horse's wrap and inspected the wound. Cleaning it off and using more of the antibiotic ointment Lexi had prescribed, he began the process of rewrapping Clover's hind leg.

"You need at least two inches of padding around the fetlock, never less but more is okay. Stay above the coronary band here." Cole pointed to the top of the hoof. "Always wrap from the outside in, applying enough pressure to hold the padding in place. It's crucial the wrap isn't tight."

Billy watched Cole intently as he wound the stretchy gauze around the pastern and then the back of the leg so the padding wouldn't move.

"Wrap the elastic gauze over the first gauze, following the same pattern." Sliding his finger in the top of the wrap, Cole explained, "Make sure you can always slip a finger between the bandage and the leg all the way around. If you can't it's too tight and you'll need to start over. An incorrect wrap can destroy a horse."

Billy nodded, angling for a better view. "Thank you."

Cole stood, "For what? Showing you something you're interested in? Look, Billy, you've been living here for six months and horses are obviously where your heart is, but I don't understand why you aren't working with Lexi or one of the other equine vets instead of shoveling out stables."

"They're only offering student internships. I can't afford to work for free, and where would I go if I didn't work here? Besides, with my past, who will want me?"

Cole returned the tote to the supply room and closed the door. Leaning against the cedar wall of the inner hallway, he regarded Billy. Turning eighteen behind bars seemed to have had a profound effect, changing the kid from reckless to responsible. What Cole knew of Billy's past was minimal, and at this point it didn't matter much. He had improved his life and kept out of trouble, barely leaving the ranch and spending most of his time in the stables.

"How long have you wanted to be an equine vet?" Billy's head shot up, eyes wide. "Don't look so surprised. Your interest is obvious, but your refusal to go on to school is confusing."

"Sir, if I may be so blunt," Billy said, "with what money? My mom's in jail and no one knows where my dad is. I need to work so I can get my own place and stop mooching off your good graces."

"At least someone around here thinks I have good graces." Cole snickered. "Your room and board is deducted from your pay, so don't think you're getting any handouts. And where school is concerned, there are financial options we can look into. Show me you're serious and I'll make sure you get what you need. You have a huge opportunity here, Billy, don't let it pass you by."

"I won't, sir," Billy said. "Tell me what you want me to do."

"First, after six months, you can stop calling me sir. Cole is fine. And I'll talk to Lexi to see if there's some program we can get you into. In the meantime, I have seven mares about to foal and I want you to be available for every one of those births. If you're going to work with horses, let's start you off from the day they enter the world. Deal?"

Cole held out his hand and Billy shook it. "Deal."

Kay waved from the porch for Cole to come to the house. After finishing with Billy, he made his way into the mudroom, prying his boots off his bare feet. A rack of buttermilk-blueberry muffins cooled on the counter, beckoning him to taste one.

"Did you have a good night's sleep?" Cole asked, helping himself to a muffin.

"Best in months." Kay set the tin in the sink to soak. "Make sure you're available tomorrow morning, and if you see Jesse before I talk to him, tell him, too. We're meeting at Jon's office at nine-thirty sharp."

"What's going on there?" Cole asked.

"I'm putting this matter of the ranch and Dance of

Hope to rest immediately." Kay opened the dishwasher door with such force it bounced back and closed. Without missing a beat, she opened it again and declared, "I'm going to put your brothers in their place once and for all. I want it on record that I will sell off every acre of this land and force the issue if I'm pushed any further. No child I gave birth to is going to deny their father's last wishes. If it wasn't for your father you boys wouldn't have a pot to pee in or a window to throw it out of, and to think—"

"Mom." Cole wrapped his arms around the animated woman. "I love you."

"I love you, too, son." Kay patted him on the back, and then suddenly pushed him away, heading toward the door. "You get in here. I have a few things I want to say to you."

Cole turned to see Chase sheepishly slide past their mother and into the kitchen.

"What are you doing here?" Cole questioned. "When I didn't see your truck I thought Tess changed your mind about going to Monkey Junction."

"Whether or not I see Ever will not change my mind, Cole." Chase looked at his mother. "I know you're disappointed, but I don't see the point of something that will cost more than it makes in the end."

"Well, I have something to change your mind," Kay began. "Tomorrow morning you make sure you're at Jon's office."

Cole didn't stay to enjoy the browbeating his brother was about to endure. If he left for Monkey Junction right away, he'd make it there before Ever's session ended.

Rain pelted the windshield when he pulled into the facility, but seeing Tess's car reassured him Ever was still here. As he ducked under the overhang near the office, Bingo greeted Cole with a firm handshake. Shorty barked and sat beside his owner, offering his paw.

"I had a feeling you'd show so I rummaged in the closet and found something from last year's Halloween party, or you can wear a tiara and boa like everyone else." Bingo leaned in the office and pulled out a garment bag. "Plum forgot I had it until Ever pulled up."

After glancing inside the bag, Cole happily thanked the man and quickly donned the outfit. The rain let up enough for him to run across to the covered area Ever was riding in.

"CC!" Ever called out as soon as she spotted him. "CC, you came!"

Standing in the doorway, Cole wore a king's crown and a deep maroon cape with white faux snow leopard trim. To his left, Tess leaned against the metal wall of the building. Surprised to see him, she nodded a greeting and gave him the briefest hint of a smile.

"Your king has arrived." Cole promenaded to the pony and bowed down before horse and rider. "At your service, Princess Ever."

"Look, Tess." Ever's doll face beamed. "CC's a king."

"I see that." Tess tried to avoid meeting his gaze.

"That means you're the queen," Ever cheered, rallying the rest of the Monkey Junction crew to join her.

"Indeed it does." Cole closed the space between him and Tess in a few short steps. "Come, my queen, our princess awaits."

Lifting Tess's hand to his mouth, he placed a light kiss below the top of her wrist and led her to the center of the makeshift ring. Ever clapped at the same time that Cole raised his left arm, inviting Tess to turn underneath it and back into his embrace. The moment instantly transported him to their senior prom when he'd wanted to kiss her in the middle of the dance floor. Scared out of his mind then, he gained the courage when he saw Ever reveling in their performance. Spinning Tess into his arm, he slowly dipped her and placed a soft kiss on her lips.

Gently returning her to an upright position, he led her back to the side of the building so Ever could continue with her therapy session. Tess held her mouth in a tight line, trying hard to fight the smile that threatened to betray her. Satisfied for the moment, Cole turned his attention fully on Ever.

Chapter Eight

Tess and Cole left Monkey Junction separately with no further contact other than the chaste kiss in front of Ever. She'd had no choice with that kiss, Tess thought. There was no way she'd risk involving the child in their emotional upheaval, and in the end, Tess knew she would have to make nice with King Cole. She giggled over the name the entire way home. Besides, if she were going to adopt Ever, Cole would definitely be a part of her life. She'd make a point of visiting the Langtrys when she and Ever visited for the holidays, certain they'd be welcome.

She spent the remainder of the day at the library, where she ran into Vicki renting a DVD on bow making. She invited Tess to join her and Miranda for a *girls only* dinner at her house since Brandon was at Double Trouble helping Jesse make some emergency fence repairs.

That night, after Vicki's delectable chicken marsala, the women retired to the living room for coffee.

"Would you mind holding the baby while I get her bottle?" Vicki gently placed Randi Lynn in Tess's arms before she could answer. "I'll be right back."

The infant smiled up at Tess with Caribbean-blue eyes. The child both mesmerized Tess and scared the daylights out of her. She was holding a tiny human in her arms. One that wouldn't remember this moment ten years from now, unlike Tess.

"I do believe she likes you." Miranda smiled. "Jesse and I are still on the fence about when we should start our family. It's been a crazy year for me and I want to feel a little more settled before we hear the pitter-patter of feet. I heard you're considering adoption, and I think that's remarkable. Do you plan to have any of your own someday?"

"I haven't thought much past Ever at this point." Tess looked down at the bundle in her arms, the thought of a baby brother or sister for Ever warming her heart.

Vicki handed Tess a baby bottle, and Randi Lynn wrapped her fingers around it, hungrily drinking the formula.

"I thought you of all people would be breast feeding," Tess said.

Vicki laughed. "That was the plan, but as I have discovered, breast feeding doesn't work for everyone. I have an extremely low supply of milk and wasn't able to provide enough nutrition for Randi Lynn. Talk about feeling like a failure. I couldn't do something women have been doing for millions of years."

"You're far from a failure," Tess said, although she understood where her friend was coming from.

"How did your research go today?" Vicki asked. "Are you leaning one way or the other?"

"I am, actually. I'm going to discuss the adoption with my father tomorrow and hear the legal side of things."

"You really are great with babies." Vicki stood and ran into the other room, returning with a camera in hand. "This will make the cutest picture."

"What are you doing?" Tess laughed quietly, careful not to disturb Randi Lynn.

Vicki snapped the photo and quickly ducked into her craft room. "I'll be right out."

"Your mommy's silly, isn't she?" Tess asked the baby. Randi Lynn stared at her in wonderment while she continued to suck on her bottle. "Where does Vicki find the energy? Speaking of high energy, how's Mable treating you? She's a force to be reckoned with, isn't she?"

"I'd be lost without her." Miranda laughed. "Would you believe she went online and got herself ordained so she could be the one to marry us? She's been down to the courthouse and everything to make sure she's all set and legal. Mable's definitely become a surrogate mother in my life since mine passed."

"I'm sorry," Tess said. "I can only imagine how rough that must have been for you. My mother filled me in on some of the details."

"All I can say is embrace the family you have, because they may not be there tomorrow." Miranda moved next to Tess on the couch. "But I believe everything happens for a reason. If my mother hadn't died, I wouldn't have bought that lottery ticket on the way home from the cemetery. I wouldn't have landed here in Texas and helped bring this little one into the world, and I certainly wouldn't have met Jesse. In the end, it's all good."

"Here you are." Vicki bounced in front of them, holding out a freshly printed photo of Tess holding Randi Lynn. "I know she's much younger than Ever, but if you have even the slightest of doubts about your ability to take care of a child, you look at this photo and see how natural you look holding a baby."

"You're too much." Tess laughed, holding the photo

in her hand. She almost didn't recognize herself. "I look relaxed."

"Foreign feeling?" Miranda asked.

"Lately it has been. Between Tim's crap and losing my job, I've felt a little…" She hesitated. *Lost* was the word Cole used last night. "Out of sorts. My routine is off and I'm not sure if I want to go back to the same thing or start over."

"Does that mean you're thinking about moving back to Ramblewood?" Vicki looked hopeful. "Feel free to babysit anytime."

"Ah, so that's all I'm good for. I see how it is." Tess held up the empty baby bottle and looked questioningly at Vicki. "What do I do now?"

"Put this on your shoulder." Vicki handed her a folded cloth. "And rest her head against you while you lightly pat her back. If she has to burp, she'll do it within the next few minutes. You've got it. So is moving back to town an option for you, and would a tall, dark and handsome cowboy have anything to do with this decision?"

"Hardly," Tess lied. "Cole Langtry is the furthest man from my mind."

"All right." Vicki nodded. "So if I told you Brandon saw you and Cole in the middle of a hot make-out session up against a tree last night, you'd tell me he dreamed the whole thing?"

"Unbelievable." Tess shook her head. "Who else saw us?"

"Everyone on the back deck of Slater's." Miranda giggled. "It's all over town."

"I thought we were far enough out of sight."

Burp.

"Aha!" Vicki shouted. A startled Randi Lynn started

to cry and Vicki reached for her daughter. "Oh, Mommy's sorry, sweetheart. So you admit there is something between the two of you."

"I'll admit there was something between us last night. There isn't today."

"Did the ol' bump and run?" Vicki giggled. "Shame on you, Tessa May."

"Will you knock it off?" Tess rose from the couch. "It was one night and I guess you could say it was a long time coming, but it doesn't matter. I'm not looking for anything serious and we all know Cole doesn't know the meaning of the word."

"Granted, Cole can be a real dog when it comes to women, but Tess, you don't know how it was when you two were together. We had to live with him pining over you day in and day out. You even took precedence over the rodeo."

"I do not believe that for one second, Vicki." Tess grabbed her bag. "But nice try. I should get going."

"Ask Brandon if you don't believe me." Vicki followed her friend to the door. "I'm telling you, Tess, that boy only rode in the rodeo because he knew it meant seeing you. His heart was never in it like Shane and Chase and that's why it was so easy for him to retire from it this year."

"Were there groupies before and after you?" Vicki went on unrelentingly. "Yes. Did he let it get out of hand? Yes, but you walked away and that's something you have to live with. But I can promise you, the entire time you were together, he was as faithful as a dog to his bone."

Tess raised both brows. "What?"

"That wasn't the best analogy, was it?" Vicki grinned.

"You know what I'm trying to say. He loved you, he never cheated on you and I'd bet he still loves you today."

"You're crazy and I must get going." Tess reached for the door.

"Well, no, actually you don't have to get going," Vicki said. "You're looking for an escape, but I understand. I want you to ask yourself one question tonight before you go to bed and I want you to sleep on the answer."

"What would that be?" Tess faced her friend.

"Do you love him?" Vicki asked. "Don't answer me and don't brush off the question. Promise me you'll think about it."

"Good night, Vic." Tess gave her friend a hug before bolting toward the door. "Miranda, it was nice getting a chance to chat with you."

Love. The biggest four-letter word there was.

Vicki's question churned in her head most of the night and she even called a few of her girlfriends back in New York to get their opinion on pursuing a relationship further than the sheets. Divided down the middle, Tess called Cheryl-Leigh for the deciding vote.

Despite the current strain in their relationship, Cheryl-Leigh was her best friend and Tess valued her advice. She conveniently left out the part about Ever since she wasn't quite sure any of her friends would understand her desire to adopt. Everyone in her close-knit circle planned to have children one day.

By the end of the night she was decidedly convinced she was not in love with Cole no matter how much her skin had prickled at his touch or how many times he invaded her thoughts during the day. Cheryl-Leigh told her to sleep on it, and the following morning when she awoke she stood firm on her answer.

Knowing her mother was already at the Magpie, Tess thought it wise to broach the subject of adoption with her father over breakfast. Ricky jumped on the bed beside her, stretching on his back legs with his front paws on her shoulder so he could rub his head against her temple, letting out soft purrs.

Following her into the bathroom, he jumped from the toilet lid to the vanity and crouched down in anticipation of fresh-running water. Their routine was the same every day. Ricky would drink from the faucet while she brushed her teeth or washed her hands. He would race her to the door, practically tripping her to guarantee his spot at the sink.

Steeling herself before she spoke to her father, she gathered her thoughts at the foot of the stairs. She ticked off every one of her speaking points, counting as she went along to make sure she included all seven.

"What are you doing?" Henry's voice boomed from the recliner near the window.

"Dad!" Tess's hand flew to her heart. "You startled me. I didn't know you were there."

"Clearly." Henry rose, folding his newspaper. "I was waiting to have breakfast with you, but if you're otherwise preoccupied with talking to yourself, we can skip it."

Smiling at the irony of the situation, Tess remembered the countless times she would sit on these very stairs, peering through the banister rails as she listened to her father prepare for trial by addressing the invisible jury in their living room. Henry had taught his daughter to always be prepared when making a case for something she strongly believed in and today she would put the lesson into practice.

"Breakfast sounds great, Dad." Tess slid her arm

through his as they walked through the house. "What are we having?"

"Cereal."

"Don't go out of your way." Tess laughed loudly.

"What do you expect?" Henry shrugged. "Your mother's the chef, not me."

Tess had to give the man credit for setting the table with two bowls, mugs, spoons and napkins. A selection of cereal boxes stood on the lazy Susan at the table's center. Choosing Cinnamon Toast Crunch, she reached for the milk.

"Dad, I want to talk to you." Tess leveled her spoon. *Timing is everything and there's no time like the present.* "I want to adopt Ever."

Henry immediately began to choke on his puffed rice, his face turning redder with every cough. Springing to his side, she slapped him on the back.

"Dad," Tess shouted. "Can you breathe?"

Henry grabbed his daughter's arm and pulled her down to his level. Clearing his throat, he said, "What are you trying to do, kill me?"

"I'm sorry." Tess slumped in the chair as her father continued to cough. Picking up her bowl, she poured the cereal down the garbage disposal. "Mom's reaction was bad enough yesterday. I thought you would be more understanding."

"Tess, sit down." Her father's voice was hoarse. "Your mother mentioned this last night, which is why I wanted to speak with you this morning."

Tess took her seat at the table, Ricky jumping in her lap.

"I'm trying to approach this realistically, Dad," she began, her voice even. "I've no intention to get married, at least not anytime soon. I'm at a point in my life where I've gotten my youth bucket list out of the way. I'm ready to settle down and roost, as the women around here say. I'm not taking this lightly, but I would like your advice from a legal standpoint."

"At least you're asking for advice." Henry shook his head. "But I'm not the right person to ask. You need to speak with someone who specializes in family law, Tess. I'm not trying to dissuade you, but I am going to ask you to be one hundred percent certain this is what you want before you begin the process, because I don't think you know fully what's involved."

"I've researched Ever's condition, and granted, I need to know more about her long-term needs, but I feel confident I have a pretty good grasp on the condition and I'm willing to take classes or talk to whoever I need to so I can learn more." Tess could feel her own conviction rising. "This is different than anything else I've wanted before. This feels right, like it's the most important thing in the world. I want this child to have a home to call her own and memories to share."

"Come into the office with me this morning. I have an early meeting, but I can introduce you to Avery Griffin. She's one of our family law attorneys and you two can set up a meeting to discuss adoption in more detail."

Excitement began to build as they drove the short distance into town. Ascending the stairs to the second-story law offices, Henry led his daughter through the richly paneled reception area. Stopping at one of the offices, he rapped lightly on the frosted glass of the open door.

"Avery." Henry stepped inside the smaller room. "This is my daughter, Tess. This is Avery Griffin, the woman with all the answers."

"I don't know about that, Hank," Avery said. "But I'll certainly try."

Hank? There was a nickname Tess hadn't heard anyone call her father other than his old high school buddies. The statuesque, champagne blonde's heather-gray wrap dress accentuated her Marilyn Monroe–like figure and Tess was fairly certain Avery was twenty years too young to have gone to school with her father. Tess heard they were bringing sexy back, but this had to be a distraction in the courtroom.

"Tess is interested in the adoption process, and when you have time, I thought we could set something up."

"I'm free now." Avery indicated the chair across from her desk. "I don't have a client for another hour. Have a seat."

"I have to run to a meeting." Henry gave his daughter a kiss on the cheek. "Thank you, Avery. Tess, we'll talk more later."

Avery eased into her hunter-green, tufted leather chair, sliding a legal pad to the center of her desk and adjusting her dark-framed glasses.

"You live in New York City, correct?" Avery started to write.

"Yes, but the little girl I want to adopt lives here." Perched on the edge of her chair, Tess clasped her hands tightly in her lap. "Not here as in Ramblewood, but here as in—well—I really don't know what town she lives in."

Avery peered over the rim of her glasses. "You don't know where she lives?"

Tess closed her eyes, trying to gather her thoughts before they came out in one jumbled mass. She was prepared to take on her family, but she wasn't quite ready for an attorney. This was all happening faster than she'd anticipated, and she remembered her notes were at the house on the nightstand.

"Ever is a four-year-old girl I met at the Monkey Junction Hippotherapy facility outside Boerne. She's in foster care and has been since she was born."

"Was Ever receiving therapy there or was she visiting?" Avery continued to write, not looking up.

"She has a mild form of cerebral palsy and she's learning how to walk with the aid of braces and crutches."

Avery tapped her pen. "Is this the same child the Langtrys are involved with?"

"Yes."

"Special girl from what I hear." Avery began to write again. "Where are you planning to live with Ever?"

"That's one of the items I wanted to discuss," Tess said. "Originally I thought New York, but I feel Ramblewood would be a better neighborhood for Ever to grow up in."

"Do you live alone?"

"Oh, no." Tess laughed, relaxing a bit in her chair. "I'm staying with my parents for the time being but I intend to get a place of my own."

"I see," Avery noted. "And employment. Where do you work?"

"I—I don't," Tess stumbled. "My company downsized and I was laid off a few weeks ago, but at the moment I'm currently looking. I'm a web designer and we're always in demand."

"I'm sure that's the case, but I don't think the state is going to look too favorably upon you as a potential adoptive parent."

"What?" Tess slumped back in the chair. "Why?"

"Do you own a car?" Avery continued.

"No, I use public transportation everywhere at home."

"Tess, it's hard to justify an adoption if you don't have a permanent place to live, whether it's New York or Texas. You need to make your living arrangements official before we move forward." Avery turned her chair slightly. "And unless you're independently wealthy, you will need to have proof of employment to show you can provide for Ever."

"I have quite a bit in savings." Tess's voice trailed off. "If I'm able to resolve those two things, do you feel I'd qualify?"

"It would be a much better start. I'm sorry, Tess." Avery walked around the desk and sat in the chair next to hers. "I know these aren't the answers you want to hear, but the way things stand today, the state won't give you a second thought. A home study is one of the first things a Child Protective Services caseworker does. There is a definite procedure in place and I can walk you through it, but presently, I'm sorry, you don't even begin to qualify. And while out-of-state adoption is allowable, in this case, it's in your best interest to stay in Texas, especially near the place where Ever receives therapy. Your family and support system are also here, making this a more favorable location."

"The sooner I declare residency in Texas, the better, then?" Changing her driver's license would be simple, and she'd get a post office box to have her mail forwarded to. There was still an open account at Ramblewood Savings & Loan. "I can do that when I leave here. And I am working for the Langtrys."

"You said you lost your job a few minutes ago." Avery leaned over her desk and retrieved her pad. "What are you doing for the Langtrys?"

"I'm designing the website and marketing plan for Dance of Hope, the hippotherapy facility they're building."

"It's my understanding that project is on hold at present," Avery said, without divulging any further details.

"Yes, but I'm sure—"

"This is a temporary position then?" Avery interrupted.

"Yes, it is." Tess's shoulders fell slightly, and she stared at the floor.

"I trust you don't have any convictions or an arrest record," Avery continued. "Because CPS will conduct a thorough background check."

"No, not even a speeding ticket."

Avery flipped the page of the pad, numbering the lines. "Declare residency, get a permanent job, a suitable place to live with handicapped access for Ever and a bedroom of her own, reference letters from friends and family recommending you for adoption, and even though it's not required by any means, it certainly helps if you're married and can provide a loving family unit. I suggest you seek out other parents of special-needs children to get a better understanding of their day-to-day lives. Being a single parent is hard enough—trust me, I live it every day. Factor in a child with cerebral palsy and the first thing a social worker is going to ask you is how you're going to handle the responsibility alone. If you haven't already, talk to Ever's foster parents. Tread carefully, though, because there is a fine line regarding what they can and can't tell you. The sooner we have a CPS worker on this case, the more information we will be able to obtain about Ever."

"The Langtrys know everything about her," Tess added.

"They are only providing for her financially." Avery jotted more notes on her pad. "Legally they don't have access to any personal information. They only provide funding for her medical expenses and even that's probably deposited into an account that can be drawn on if necessary. They'll never actually see any of the bills."

"This is so confusing." Tess unfolded her hands and perched on the edge of her seat.

"That's what we are here for." Avery tore off the page and handed it to Tess. "Let's start with the basics and we'll move on from here."

"I can handle everything except the marriage part." Tess laughed nervously. "But I'll cover the rest of these issues over the next few days."

"I appreciate your enthusiasm, but this isn't an easy process and it won't happen overnight. I can assure you of that. Have a detailed plan ready to present to a CPS caseworker." Avery stood, signaling the end of their meeting. "The state doesn't take this lightly, and again I stress to you, the process takes time. There will be many meetings and home studies and supervised visits. And you have quite a bit of groundwork to cover. They will expect you to be well established here before you're approved, but at least we can start the process once you get those items under control."

"Thank you." Tess held out her hand. "What do I owe you?"

"Are you kidding me?" Avery laughed, shaking Tess's hand. "Nothing. This is what we do here. We help each other's families out when they need it. I owe your father after the mess he got my mother out of last year. Seriously, Tess, take everything I'm saying as gospel and get to work. Come see me when you have your case in order."

Avery handed Tess her card and walked her out through the reception area.

"Thank you, Avery."

Out on the street, Tess remembered she had left her car at the house. Deciding the walk would do her good and give her some time to think, she headed for the Magpie. Her hand on the door to the luncheonette, she hesitated and looked toward Shelby Street.

The cool fall air caused her to pull her coat tighter around her as she walked toward the post office a few blocks down. There she rented a box and filled out a permanent forwarding order for her mail. Although Avery hadn't told her exactly what she wanted to hear, Tess wasn't going to let a few checklist items stop her from adopting Ever. She felt all the events leading up to this day were a sign she was ready for the commitment.

Tess doubled back to the real estate office and made an appointment to sit down with Bond Gallo to see what was available in town. She knew the bank wouldn't give her a loan without a job but she was hoping to rent something in the meantime, even if it meant paying for the entire year up front to prove financial security.

By noon, Tess had successfully changed the address on her credit and bank accounts. The bank in New York was emailing her the forms to transfer her accounts to Ramblewood Savings & Loan and this afternoon she planned to head to the motor vehicles department and change her driver's license.

She called Monkey Junction and asked if they knew of any parents who would be willing to talk to her. Eileen told her she would make some inquiries on her behalf.

Tess needed to tell Cheryl-Leigh she was leaving New York. She felt she owed it to her friend to give her the earliest notice possible to find a new roommate, but she didn't feel the middle of the day when she was at work was right. It could wait until the weekend. Today she needed to find a job herself. Avery was right. Working for the Langtrys was temporary, and right now, the best place for Tess to be was where she was needed most and most qualified—at the Magpie.

Marriage. It was the last item on Avery's list and an instant reminder of her conversation with Chase yesterday morning. She still found it impossible to believe Cole had intended to propose to her. It did clarify why Shane had a sudden inexplicable animosity for her. Marriage was the last thing on her mind two years ago. It was something she hadn't considered with Cole or anyone else. Tess never saw herself as the marrying kind until Tim proposed, and when he did, it seemed like the next most logical step in their relationship.

But Cole and his wild, wanton ways? Tess didn't think it was possible to tame him, which was why she was so hesitant to start dating him in the first place.

Tess obliterated *marriage* from Avery's list. It was *not* an option.

JON REESE SAT behind the mahogany desk of his new private practice office, courtesy of the generous compensation Joe had given him. Cole, Jesse and Kay sat to the right, a sense of calm about them that seemed to have noticeably set Shane on edge, his foot tapping wildly. Henry sat next to him and looked half-ready to saw Shane's leg off if he didn't stop soon. Chase hung near the door like a young steed ready to bolt the minute the pasture gate opened.

"Thank you for coming here today," Jon began. "I wanted to bring this matter to everyone's attention before I file a motion with the court. Kay has the legal right to terminate the lease agreement with Bridle Dance at any given time. The lease was open-ended, with no restrictions. She owns the land, therefore giving her ultimate control on how it's used."

"That doesn't mean she can force us to use it for Dance of Hope, does it?" Chase asked.

"No, but it does mean she can sell part or all of the land to finance Dance of Hope if she desires," Jon responded.

"Sell the land?" Shane leaned forward. "That would mean the end of Bridle Dance and the Langtry legacy."

"You and Chase have two choices." Kay matched her son's stare. "You either use some of Bridle Dance's money to build Dance of Hope, or I will sell however much of *my land* as I need to bankroll it myself. You can run the business at Double Trouble, because it doesn't matter to me. The choice is yours, but I assure you, Dance of Hope will be built as your father planned and that's final. And it will be his legacy."

Everyone's attention was on Shane, but he made no move to speak.

Jesse turned toward Chase. "Are you going to let him destroy everything Dad worked for out of stubborn pride and greed? You can end this, Chase, today."

"I call your bluff," Shane said, before Chase answered. "You'll never let Bridle Dance go like that. You'd break Dad's heart."

"You already have, son." Kay stood, walked over to Shane and lifted his chin. "I'm so disappointed in you for the way you've acted these past few months. Your father would rather watch Bridle Dance die than see his children behave this way. You may have lived a privileged life, but you weren't raised with dollar signs in your eyes. If greed is what you're about, then I aim to take everything you took for granted away."

"Henry, can Mom really do this?" Chase asked.

"Yes, she can," Henry said. "If one or both of you don't go along with your father's plans, it will be the end of Bridle Dance."

"Isn't that blackmail?" Shane asked.

"The courts won't see it that way," Jon said. "Your mother is exercising her right to sell any portion of the land she chooses and she is fully within her legal rights to do so. She only needs a handful of acres to run Dance of Hope."

"You win." Chase threw his hands in the air. "I vote for Dance of Hope."

Wordlessly, Kay pulled Chase into an embrace while dabbing at her eyes. Shane stormed out of the office, not willing to admit defeat. At the same time Henry rose to shake Jon's hand.

"Well played, solicitor," Henry said. "I won't ask if Kay was seriously considering selling the land. I'll just say things worked out the way Joe would have wanted."

"Where do we go from here?" Cole asked. "Can we break ground?"

"Chase, if you'll step over here and sign this, we will officially have a majority vote to build Dance of Hope." Jon shuffled through the papers on his desk and asked his paralegal to step in to notarize the signatures.

By the end of the meeting, Dance of Hope was free and clear to move forward. Outside in the parking lot Cole called the general contractor for the facility to see if he could set everything in motion right away.

Watching his mother walk out of Jon's office with Jesse and Chase by her side was bittersweet. Nicolino was right about Shane feeling the entire family had turned against him. Cole wanted to win this battle for his father, but he didn't want to alienate his brother in the process.

Chase ran to catch up with Cole. "I don't know how to tell you this, so I'll come right out with it. I told Tess about Vegas."

"Told her what about Vegas?" Cole clenched his fist. "What did you tell her?"

"Everything. The proposal, the wedding date, everything."

Grabbing his brother by the shirt, Cole slammed him into the side of his truck. "You had no right." Cole couldn't believe his brother had betrayed him. Jon and Jesse tried to step between them when Chase rose up and spun his brother around, forcing Cole back over the hood of the truck.

"Tess wants to adopt Ever, and if you'd swallow that pride of yours for a moment, maybe you could adopt her together."

Cole immediately released his hold on his brother, allowing Chase to step aside. "What did she say?"

"What is going on around here?" Kay asked.

"Come on, Mom." Jesse led her to his truck. "I'll fill you in on the way home."

"Not a whole lot." Chase straightened out his shirt and readjusted his jacket. "She was more surprised than anything. She didn't know you were that serious about her, but she listened."

"I meant what'd she say concerning Ever?" Cole knew there was no sense in trying to rehash the whole proposal memory. It was a mistake, plain and simple, better left in the past. He wished his brother had done just that. Chase's lack of judgment would only increase Cole's awkwardness with Tess when it was already at an all-time high. With Dance of Hope moving forward, he needed her to ramp up her marketing plans immediately.

"She's been on a fact-finding mission relating to Ever's type of cerebral palsy. I believe her exact words were along the lines of she wants Ever to have a loving and normal home where she can make memories and feel secure when she goes to bed at night."

"So Tess plans on moving back to Ramblewood?" Cole asked.

"I'm not going to be your go-between." Chase turned away. "Why don't you talk to her and find out?"

The last thing Cole wanted today was Tess bombarding him with a million questions about Vegas. Dance of Hope was on its way to becoming a reality and it deserved to be front and center. It also deserved a celebration. But somehow a celebration seemed lost without Tess.

Chapter Nine

Cole drove through town, slowing his truck in front of the Magpie to check if Tess was there. Not seeing her car, he proceeded on to her house. Tess wanting to adopt Ever didn't surprise him the way he thought it should have, and he had to admit that after seeing her with Ever, Cole easily envisioned Tess as her mother.

It was her constant career-focused agenda that thwarted those trying to get close to her. How Tim managed to pin her down for two years was beyond him, but in the end, he ran off with someone else, so it wasn't the blissful love affair Maggie had made it out to be.

Cole definitely saw Tess fitting into the mother role. But with Ever? He'd always envisioned the little girl on his ranch with a hippotherapy facility in her own backyard. There was no doubt he could provide a better life for Ever than Tess. Convincing the state to allow him to adopt her would be an uphill battle and he hadn't expected to fight the woman he—

"Don't even think it," Cole said to himself. "It will only make matters worse."

Seeing Tess open her car door to get in, Cole beeped his horn and parked his truck at the end of her driveway, preventing her from leaving. He mentally smiled, noting Tess's frustration when she realized she was unable to back out. Irritating her was fast becoming one of his favorite hobbies.

He climbed out of his truck. "We won," Cole called to her. "Chase relented this morning and crossed over to our side. Dance of Hope is a go."

Tess tossed her bag in the car and ran down the driveway, allowing Cole to pull her into a tight embrace. *This is right.* The moment she stepped into his arms, he knew this was where she belonged.

"I am so proud of you!" Tess squealed. "This must be a huge weight lifted off you. You're finally realizing your father's dream. Congratulations."

"Sort of." Cole reluctantly released her, but intertwined his pinky in hers. It was something they used to do when they were kids. "We won because Mom threatened to sell the land in order to finance the facility if Shane and Chase didn't vote our way. I honestly didn't have anything to do with it. Mom pulled rank."

"How can you say you had nothing to do with it, Cole?" Tess shifted to stand in front of him, barely grazing his chest with hers. "I saw your plans. You put a lot of your heart and soul into this project. You should be proud."

"You mean my father's plans. I've merely been the executor of his wishes, Tess. None of this is mine, and that's fine by me. This is my father's heart and soul, and somewhere along the line, I guess it became mine. But I can't take credit for any of it."

"Well, you can take credit in knowing that Ever will have Dance of Hope to come to whenever she wants to." Tess grinned. "I sort of have news of my own. I spoke to an attorney this morning, and I've decided to try to adopt Ever."

"You've already seen an attorney?" Cole stiffened. She was one step ahead of him.

"Avery Griffin. She was very enlightening, to say the least. I have some things to work out first, but once I do, I'm going to formally begin the process."

"What do you need to work out?" Cole asked, wondering if he played in any part of her decision.

"Declaring residency here, which I took care of today, and getting a job and a place to live."

Cole's heart skipped a beat at the confirmation she wouldn't be heading back to New York.

"I thought you out of anyone would be thrilled." Tess frowned. "Why don't you look happy about this? Let me guess, you side with my mother in thinking I would be horrible at raising a child."

"Maggie said that?" Cole didn't think the woman had it in her to be so heartless to anyone, let alone her own daughter.

"She might as well have." Tess slid her hands into the back pocket of her jeans and averted her gaze. "She laughed at me in front of your mom, Mable and Vicki just at the thought of it."

His mother knew about this? Why hadn't she said anything to him?

"Is that why you flew out of the house the other day doing Mach one away from the ranch?"

"I left because I had adoption and cerebral palsy research to do and plans to make." Tess clenched her jaw. "I want to give Ever the happiness and family she needs and deserves."

At Tess's response, Cole wanted to pull her into his arms, kiss her madly and make love to her again. In a bed. Tess was home to stay and Cole wanted to make her his forever.

"Woo-hoo!" Tess said. "Are you with me?"

"I'm sorry, I have a lot on my mind." That was the understatement of the year. Cole climbed in his truck to hide the evidence of his growing arousal. The fact that they'd had sex in this very vehicle less than twenty-four hours ago added to his growing need. "Come out to the ranch and celebrate with us. We have a lot to go over for the website. I want to document the entire process from breaking ground to opening day and it would give you a chance to show off some of your photography skills. My dad would have loved that."

Tess stood motionless on the sidewalk. She didn't say the words, but he knew she wanted to ask him about Vegas and he wanted to discuss last night.

"All right, let's get this out of the way, although the end of your driveway wasn't exactly where I envisioned this conversation."

"Do you want to come in?" Tess offered.

"Yeah, give me a minute." Cole needed a chance to regain his composure and cool his desire for her. "I have to make a few quick phone calls."

A few minutes later, Cole trudged up the stairs and joined Tess. Instead of the porch swing where they would have been closer and more comfortable, Tess balanced her backside on the railing, leaving him to lean against the clapboards of the house. Pumpkins and pots of orange and yellow mums decorated the decking, while hanging baskets of ferns offered some privacy from the street. If he snuck a kiss, chances were none of the neighbors would be the wiser.

Cole began to move toward her but hesitated when she opened her mouth to speak. Resting his head against the house, he closed his eyes, bracing himself for the onslaught hurtling his way.

"Why didn't you tell me?" Tess asked. "I shouldn't have heard it from Chase."

"No, you shouldn't have," Cole agreed. "It wasn't his place to say anything."

"Don't you think I deserved to know?"

Cole laughed. "Honestly, no. After the way you tore out of there, I didn't feel I owed you any explanations. I know my track record isn't great with women, but for you to assume I cheated on you made me so—it pissed me off, Tess. I never once thought about cheating on you."

"Oh, okay." Tess nodded. "And you never bedded any of those women we ran into that night?"

"Well, I—"

"Spare me the details, Cole, because one night in New York you were so drunk, you proceeded to tell the entire bar how many groupies you've dipped into while on the road."

While he didn't remember saying the words in front of Tess, conquest bragging after too much Jim Beam was his downfall. He wasn't about to deny the truth and it was too late for apologies. He never meant to hurt her.

"I knew your reputation when we got together. Hell, I witnessed it firsthand every time I visited you on the road over the years. It's the main reason I kept everything on a friendship level."

Tess slid off the rail and stepped closer. "But I'm not going to lie to you. It was constantly on my mind every time you were out of town. I sat in the stands with the other rodeo wives and girlfriends. I've heard all the stories and I know some cowboys are straight-up respectable and don't mess around on the road and then there are others that take anything with a pulse to bed. But I couldn't pretend it didn't bother me, Cole. This is about me and how I felt that night. I flew across the country to see you and I had to listen to some women ask when you were going to screw them again. That sure as hell didn't make me feel good about us. I'm far from a prude, Cole, but how much is someone supposed to take?"

"But I didn't—"

"Dammit, Cole, they are a product of your environment. You are responsible because your actions brought them there. They were like Pavlov's dogs looking for another bone."

"If you never fully trusted me, why did you move forward with the relationship?" Cole was growing more disgusted with himself for the way he'd acted and for hurting the one woman he truly loved. He used to keep count of the number of women he'd been with. It was a competition between him and Shane, but one that stopped the moment he'd started dating Tess. "You didn't give us a fair chance."

"I wanted to." Tess looked up at him. "I didn't realize how serious you were until Chase told me you were going to return to New York with me and stay until I went home for Christmas. I would never have believed you were going to give up the rodeo and the ranch to live with me in the city. You'd wither up and die there."

"I knew I wanted you and that's all that mattered." The decision to leave the rodeo was easy to make. The lifestyle was starting to get to him and his body was in a constant state of pain. After so many injuries, settling down and starting a family was very enticing. But he had never fully committed to leaving the ranch. His hope had been to convince Tess to return home with him, but he never thought it the whole way through.

Figuring their future would work itself out, Cole ran with his emotions and planned the elaborate proposal.

"Neither one of us was ready for marriage," Tess declared. "Wow, two years—it seems like a lifetime ago, doesn't it? I mean, so much has changed. I had these huge career plans and never envisioned leaving the city. Now, here I am, and New York feels like it's a million miles away."

She gave a rueful shrug. "A career is one thing, but when it's gone, it's truly gone. You can't curl up with it at night and you can't call it when something's bothering you. I thought New York was the life I wanted. I tried it, I succeeded and then I lost my job and…well, it's not for me anymore. I'd like the opportunity to be a mother to Ever and be back home surrounded by my family and friends."

"Come with me." Cole grabbed Tess's hand and led her down the stairs before she could protest. I want to show you something.

THEY RODE TO Bridle Dance in peaceful silence, not feeling the need to talk. Leaving him in Vegas still stung, but Cole understood her reasons behind it. He also realized they weren't anywhere near ready for marriage then and he'd just got caught up in the romance of the idea. Fast forward to today. They were older, more grounded and both had a common goal in mind—to give Ever a home of her own.

Pulling up in front of one of the abandoned ranch cottages, Cole jumped down and met Tess on the passenger side.

"Wow, I forgot these places existed." Tess bounced up the two-step porch and peered in the windows. "Is this Hope's Cottage?"

"Sure is. It's the original homestead that Mom and Dad lived in briefly when they were first married, until they built the main house." He opened the door, the rusted hinges squealing from lack of use. "It's almost unrecognizable. It really is a shame it's been left to rot out here."

Tess walked around, noting every crevice. The house had great bones, with an open floor plan, modern for its time, but years of neglect had really taken its toll on the old place. "It's amazing when you think about it. I remember your mom telling the story of your great-grandfather building this house and giving it to your great-grandmother for a wedding present. That truly is one of the most romantic gestures. Hope's Cottage. You should restore this place."

"That was the plan. The first son to marry was slated to get this house, but no one wanted to tackle the renovations. When Shane married Sharon, there was no way in hell she was going to live in a cottage when she had her sights on the main house. Jesse has Double Trouble with Miranda, so that leaves the next Langtry in line."

"It could be so beautiful." Tess walked from room to room, stopping in what must be the master bedroom.

"Mom and Dad would get so mad at us kids for coming up here. The windowpanes are original to the house and if we ever broke one of them, they would have had our head on a skewer. I love how you can see the waves in the glass from the manufacturing process in the late eighteen hundreds."

"You know a lot of this can be salvaged and restored."

Cole wrapped his arms around Tess and turned her toward him. "And us? Can we be salvaged and restored?"

THE MOMENT HIS lips met hers Tess knew she was a goner. An overwhelming desire to settle into his arms and agree to whatever he said washed over her. She returned his kiss and deepened the passion, trying to find every last ounce of restraint before things progressed to where they had last night in his pickup.

"Wait a second, cowboy." Tess's breath sounded ragged even to herself. "I have to focus on one thing at a time and Ever is my top priority."

Cole released her and ran his hands over his face. "You'll make a great mother."

"You almost sound hesitant." There was a hint of disappointment in his voice, but Tess wasn't sure if it was because she'd broken their kiss or because he had doubts about her and Ever. "Do you really have faith in me?"

"I think you can do whatever you put your mind to." Cole brushed a dust bunny from her hair, resisting the urge to lean in for another kiss. "You said you need a job."

"I can waitress at the Magpie." Tess wandered into the kitchen and ran her hands over the old wooden counters. "Okay, these would have to be replaced. They've been short a waitress for quite a while and it will free up Mom to do her catering. That seems to be her thing lately."

"Or you could work at the ranch as the marketing director," Cole said, from the doorway.

"Marketing director?" Tess had difficulty squelching her delight. "You're seriously offering me a permanent position? What happened to your brothers' approval? Don't I have to be voted in or something like that?"

"Executive decision." Cole smirked. "There's nothing wrong with waitressing, but your heart doesn't belong there. Do what you love and come work with me. The pay's a whole lot better."

"Yes!" Tess threw her arms around his neck and kissed him, pulling away before things became too serious. "This might be a problem, though. If we're working together, we can't be doing…you know."

"You'll barely see me during the day." Cole set her away from him. "So you won't be tempted to ravage me."

"Oh, there's a laugh." Not far from the truth, but a laugh just the same. "I promise to control myself, Mr. Langtry. I need to find a house. Avery said it had to have access for Ever in order to pass the home study. I didn't think the bank would give me a mortgage and I dread renting, but if you give me a contract of some sort, it would show job security to the state and the bank. And maybe I would be able to buy something. I have an appointment to meet with Bond—"

"I have a better idea." Cole advanced to Tess, bending down on one knee. "Marry me and live here."

Tess reached for the counter to steady herself. She opened her mouth to speak but nothing came out.

"This is the reason I brought you here. This house is perfect for Ever, don't you see? It's on one floor and I can easily build a ramp out front, although at the rate she's going, she'll be up and down those few stairs soon enough. And yes, it's far from the ranch house, but the main ranch road leads straight here, so we're not isolated."

"Are you seriously proposing to me?" Tess asked. "Cole, I don't know what to say."

"Look around, Tess." Cole sprang to his feet and led Tess around the room. "Can't you see us here, raising our little girl?"

Tess easily envisioned Ever playing in the living

room while she cooked dinner. Maybe she'd have a garden of her own. Ever would have access to horses whenever she wanted and Tess would practically be working from home. It really was an incredible setup. But marriage? Was she ready to settle down with the man before her?

"I have to admit, it is pretty wonderful."

"So you'll marry me?" Cole dropped down to the floor again, causing Tess to giggle.

"I—"

"What are you two doing in here?" Shane entered the kitchen and saw Cole on one knee. "Don't tell me you've decided to propose again? Be careful, big brother, Tess has a tendency to bolt. She'd be good in a remake of that movie *Runaway Bride*. She kind of looks like Julia Roberts with shorter hair, but you're no Richard Gere."

"Shane, get the hell out of here." Cole stood and faced off against his brother. "I don't want to fight with you."

"Too late for that, big bro." Shane jabbed at Cole's chest with his finger. "You, Mom and Jesse may have won, but I want no part of it. I don't want any part of you or anyone else in this pathetic family."

"Have you been drinking?" Cole asked, leaning in to sniff his brother. Shane took a shot at him, but Cole grabbed his fist before it connected with his chin.

"No, I haven't been drinking." Shane struggled against Cole. "I'm afraid if I do I might show you how I really feel. Is this who you want to marry, Tess? A bully who throws his weight around, then gets Mommy to fight his battles?"

Cole shoved Shane backward. "I did no such thing. Mom won this battle on her own, but it was one that could have been avoided from the beginning if you weren't so selfish and greedy."

"Enough!" Tess yelled. "You're both selfish, stubborn and greedy and you should be ashamed of yourselves. If you're going to fight, take it outside so you don't go and break something in this house, like one of those windows I heard so much about a minute ago. Then again, you two deserve the wrath of Kay. Fighting like this is crazy. You're both impossible and I feel sorry for anyone who has to be around you."

"He's the jackass," Cole said.

"You both are!" Tess shouted. "Your desire to beat one another has made you completely blind to the obvious solution and I don't know why none of us thought of it sooner."

"Which is?" Shane demanded.

"You two could have it both ways if you loosened your grips a little. There is no reason why you can't showcase the spirit of the horse in both a rodeo school *and* a therapy facility. Cole, your plans won't be nearly as elaborate as you thought, but you would still have an award-winning facility. And Shane, you and Chase would finally have the school you wanted even though it may not have every item on your wish list. And I bet if you worked it out properly, you'd even cut costs by sharing some of the buildings."

Dumbfounded, the brothers gave Tess their full attention, but her head was swimming too wildly to continue. She needed to think about Cole's proposal and then she might be able to help them sort out this mess about the ranch's future. "I've had enough for the day," she announced. "I'm driving the truck back to my house. You can pick it up later." She shot them both a contemptuous glance as she headed out the door. "Besides, you two deserve to be saddled together."

Chapter Ten

Tess arrived home for dinner with her parents. All this time she'd been back in Ramblewood and it was the first night they'd managed to have a meal together.

"There you are," Maggie said. "Your father and I couldn't figure out where you were since your car was in the driveway. I went ahead and fed Ricky."

"I was out at the ranch and you didn't have to do that. He doesn't normally eat until later." Tess knew her mother was simply trying to help. "I'm sorry, thank you for thinking of him."

"I didn't see you at the main house." Maggie poured three glasses of water from the water filtration pitcher and placed them on the table. "And yes, I did have to feed Ricky. I made tuna noodle casserole and it was the only way I kept him from jumping on the counter."

Tess rubbed her feline companion behind the ears. "I'm sure Ricky was very grateful."

"So grateful he jumped in the sink and tried to drink out of the faucet." Maggie waggled her finger at the tabby purring against Tess's calf. "Really, Tess, that's a horrible habit you've taught him. I hope you're still planning to make time to help me with the shower tomorrow."

"Sure, what do you need me to do?" Tess asked.

"I need you to get some sort of a mat or at least put newspaper down in front of his litter box. I thought you brought one with you the last time," Maggie added. "I've bent my no-cats rule for Ricky, but he's tracking litter throughout the house. Teach him to wipe his paws."

"I meant what do you need me to do for the shower." Henry and Tess giggled at her mother's scattered thoughts. "And I did buy a mat, but it wasn't in the attic with the litter box. I'll pick up another one tomorrow."

"Oh, is that what that rubber, knobby thing was in the attic," Henry said, rising from the table. "I'll check the cellar because I may have moved it there."

"You're on cupcake-decorating duty tomorrow."

Taking the casserole from the oven and setting it on the stove top to cool a bit, Maggie joined her daughter at the table while Henry dashed down the basement stairs.

"Your father told me you met with Avery this morning."

"Are you going to laugh at me again?" Tess asked, unable to hide the sarcasm and hurt in her voice. "Really, Mom, I'm not going to discuss this with you if you're going to mock me."

"Actually, I was going to commend you for wanting to take on such a huge responsibility." Maggie reached for her daughter's hand, then seemed to think better of it and returned to the stove.

"What, Mom? You can't touch me now?" Tess asked. "I remember when I used to get a hug from you every day. Now I get one the day I arrive and the day I leave and that's all. Am I that much of a disappointment to you?"

Hurt reflected in Maggie's eyes. "I never know the

right thing to do with you anymore. If I hug you, then I'm being condescending and pacifying you, but if I don't, then I'm criticized again. Honestly Tess, you've become a real pain in the ass."

"Me? Mom, you have done nothing but judge me since the moment I got here. I listen to you sing the praises of a stranger, yet when it comes to me, you laugh or you tell me I can't do something. I don't get it."

"Because you're my daughter and you're not living up to your potential."

Maggie dropped the casserole in the center of the lazy Susan, causing it to slosh over the side. "Henry, either get up here to dinner or I'm feeding it to the cat."

"I'm right here, Maggie. You don't have to yell." Henry sat in his chair at the head of the table and looked as if he was trying to figure out why the casserole was so lopsided. Reaching underneath the turntable, he reset the top on the bearings and tested it to make sure it rotated easily. Maggie smacked his hand with the spatula she was using to fling crescent rolls onto their plates. "I was trying to straighten— Oh, never mind. What did Tess do now?"

"Nothing," Tess grumbled. "It's apparently what I haven't done with my life. I'll have you know I've accomplished more than most women my age."

"That's not what I meant, Tess," Maggie said. "Since high school everything has been centered on your career and how you can move up the corporate ladder. Family took second place. Even Tim took second place with you."

"Maggie, give her a chance." Henry hid his hands under the table in fear of another swat. "Stop trying to live her life for her."

Tess balled up her napkin and threw it on the table. "I'm done here."

"Aw, honey, don't leave." Maggie met Tess on the other side of the table. "It's not that I don't think you're capable of raising a child. I just want *you* to be sure *you're* ready for one, especially one with special needs."

"There's no perfect time, Mom, and I have so much to offer Ever. Yes, it's going to be difficult and I'm sure there will be heartache like there is with all children, but that's okay. I've written the book on perfection when it comes to my career and relationships and we all know how that turned out. Each day will be a learning experience for Ever and myself, so I'm asking you to please support me on this."

Maggie dabbed her eyes. "I really am proud of you."

They ate dinner and her parents were thrilled when Tess told them she'd decided to move back to Ramblewood. But after Tess explained Avery's checklist, Henry warned her not to get her hopes up too high when it came to the whole adoption process.

"From what I understand, it can take up to a year, sometimes longer, depending on the situation."

"Avery said the average was six months, but they must make some allowance for children with special needs, right?" Tess asked.

"I would think those cases would take longer," Maggie added. "They need to insure these children aren't put in any danger."

"Well, I'm going to watch the news." Henry excused himself from the table. "Dinner was delicious, dear."

Tess admired her parents' relationship. It wasn't flawless by any means, but they seemed to balance each other. Where her father could be a little gruff, Maggie made up for it with sugary kindness. Where

her father tended to be overly generous with some of
their charities, Maggie watched every cent they spent.
Arguments were the norm, but they never went to bed
mad at each other. Tess thought that was a silly sen-
timent reserved for television shows from the fifties
like *Father Knows Best* or *I Love Lucy,* but it seemed
to work for her parents.

"Cole asked me to marry him today."

Silence.

Expecting at least some form of response from her
mother, Tess said, "Mom, did you hear me?"

Maggie barely nodded in acknowledgment, remaining frozen in place at the sink, her hands still holding
the dish she'd removed from the table.

Tess snickered. "Maggie Dalton, speechless. I never
thought I'd see the day. And you can relax, Mom, I
didn't accept."

"You what?" Well, that silence was short-lived. "How
could you turn that boy down?"

"I didn't say I turned him down. I didn't give him
an answer yet." Despite Shane barging into the room
and ruining the moment, Tess thought it was sweet the
way Cole had proposed to her the old-fashioned way, on
one knee. Vegas would have been flashy and dramatic,
but there was something innocent and charming about
a proposal in the very house his great-grandfather had
built and given to his great-grandmother on their wedding day. Tess only wished she had been able to give
him an answer before Shane walked in. Now she wondered if he was only caught up in the moment and asked
her because he wanted to adopt Ever himself. They
never even said the words *I love you* to each other. But
she did love him, didn't she?

"Let's hear the details." Maggie dried her hands on

the dish towel dangling from her apron. "When did you two become so serious all of a sudden?"

Tess confessed her reckless night with Cole, sparing her mother the details. Maggie would be horrified if she knew her daughter was getting it on with the town's most eligible bachelor in the front seat of his pickup in a public parking lot, no less.

Afraid Maggie would chastise her, Tess was surprised when she said, "It's about time!"

"Excuse me?" Tess glanced into the living room to make sure her father hadn't overheard the conversation, but Henry was asleep in his recliner, head back, mouth open. "This isn't the reaction I thought I'd get from you."

"Why not?" Maggie lifted her chin. "I'm no prude. Your father and I were together before we got married."

"No, no, no." Tess stuck her fingers in her ears, shaking her head. "I don't need the gritty details of your sex life before or after you and Daddy got married."

Maggie pulled her daughter's hands away from her head. "I understand what it's like, but I still don't know why you didn't accept."

Tess filled her mother in on why she had broken up with Cole in Vegas two years ago, including Chase's admission about Cole's planned proposal. And when she thought her mother wouldn't be able to absorb another ounce of her Langtry drama, Tess told Maggie about the house and how Shane interrupted the proposal.

"I don't know what to do about Cole. How do I know he asked me for me and not because of Ever?"

Maggie refreshed their coffees before reaching into the refrigerator and removing a bottle of Baileys Irish Cream, adding a healthy shot to each of their cups.

"Shh, don't tell your father. He'd kill us if he knew we drank his Baileys."

"I won't." Tess giggled. "I promise."

"You said Shane walked in on Cole's proposal, so when are you going to give the man an answer?"

"I don't want to get hurt again, Mom." It wasn't even a month ago that she was engaged to someone else and planning a spring wedding. "I don't want to rush into anything just because it would help Ever's adoption. She needs to come first, and a year down the road, we'll see what happens with Cole. Although I do have to admit, living on the ranch in that house would be the best place for Ever."

"Honey, I think you need to realize there is such a thing as too much independence," Maggie said. "You alienate yourself from the rest of the world with your constant focus on yourself and your goals."

"What?" Tess was offended. "I do not."

"Let me ask you something, who are your real friends?"

"That's a silly question." Tess pursed her lips. "I have more friends than I know what to do with. I was planning on twelve bridesmaids at my wedding."

"Half of those were Tim's relatives and the other half were your college sorority sisters. You whined more than once that you felt obligated to include them." Maggie grabbed a magnetic notepad from the side of the refrigerator and tossed it on the table in front of Tess, along with a pen. "Write down the names of your true friends, the ones you've told about adopting Ever."

Tess held the pen, rolling it between her fingers. She wrote Cole's name at the top. Next she wrote Vicki and Chase. Tess slammed the pen down on the table. "This doesn't prove anything, Mother. So I've only told a few people. So what?"

"You're missing the point." Maggie circled Cole's name. "No matter where you've been or whatever the situation was, Cole's been your one true constant and that man's waited for you his entire life. Don't expect him to keep waiting."

Leave it to her mother to find a way to squeeze in a guilt trip. By the end of the night Tess was completely talked out. Knowing she needed to apprise Cheryl-Leigh of her plans, she picked up the phone and dialed her friend.

By the end of the conversation Tess learned two things. Cheryl-Leigh thought Tess would make a great mother and she had officially got the promotion Tess had wanted. Cheryl-Leigh told her she didn't need to get a roommate—*of course not with the bonus and salary increase she received*—and if something changed and Tess wanted to come back, the apartment door would always be open.

Maggie was wrong. Cheryl-Leigh was officially added to the list of true friends.

The hour was late, too late to call Cole. Tess hoped he wouldn't remain upset with her for walking out on him earlier. Although, according to Shane, that was her trademark move. Tess always knew she was a runner, but she considered herself someone who ran *to* something, not someone who ran away from her problems.

Besides, Cole and Shane needed that time alone to talk and sort themselves out after the long battle. It had been a hard few months for the Langtrys. Instead of trying to outwit each other, Kay included, they needed to come together now and work with one another.

Funny, Tess laughed to herself. Maybe she should

take some of her own advice and accept Cole's proposal. It would give her an instant edge with the state adoption agency. If only he had begun with *I love you,* she would know how he truly felt without doubting it was only because of Ever.

Tess drifted off to sleep until Maggie knocked on her door at three-thirty in the morning.

"Tess, honey," her mother whispered. "You said you'd help me this morning. We have a lot to do before I open the luncheonette."

Showered and ready in record time, Tess met her mother by the front door. They drove behind the Magpie, where the two catering vans her mother had rented for the week were parked. Inside the luncheonette, Tess flicked the lights on in the kitchen while Maggie removed trays of cupcakes from the walk-in for Miranda's bridal shower later that afternoon. Slicing a cupcake open, Maggie tested it to insure they hadn't dried out overnight.

Tess gathered the ingredients for her mother's signature buttercream recipe. Sifting the powdered sugar, Maggie added it and the almond extract to the Kitchen-Aid mixer. Most bakeries used vanilla extract and milk for their buttercream recipes, but Maggie liked to mix things up a bit by substituting almond flavoring and using half-and-half for a more decadent frosting. Always working in small batches, she tailored each tint using various pods of gel coloring.

Handing Tess a prefilled pastry bag, Maggie instructed her to pipe out twenty-five roses of each color. Tess had never mastered frosting a cake, but roses and rosebuds were her specialty. She piped the pale pink and red buttercream onto the pastry nail, spinning it between her thumb and forefinger, creating beautiful pink roses with scarlet highlights.

The luncheonette was busy but the afternoon's closing finally approached. Maggie, Bridgett and Tess were beat and Bert was just beet-red. He maintained that you could always tell the food was ready when your face turned redder than the meat. Bridgett had handled most of the after-lunch customers alone so Maggie and Tess could finish the preparations for the bridal shower.

With no time to run home, Tess changed into clothes she'd brought with her and touched up her makeup in the bathroom.

"Wow," Bert said, when she emerged from the bathroom in a sleeveless, cream-colored floral party dress, with a fifties flare to the skirt. "You sure do clean up nice."

"Thank God for Estée Lauder," Tess said.

"Who's Essie Waters?" Bert asked.

"Never mind, old man." Maggie pushed Bert aside to get a better view of her daughter. "You look very pretty, dear. Can we expect a formal announcement later?"

"Mother!" Tess giggled. "I don't know what I'm going to say when I see him, but I promise, you'll be the first to know."

WITH THE BRIDAL shower in full swing, Cole and his brothers kept themselves and the horses a good distance from the house since there was nothing like a shrieking female to spook a horse.

Surprised to see Lexi's truck near the stable, Cole strode in to see what was keeping her from the bridal festivities. Standing in red stilettos and what he would describe as a *little* black dress, Lexi made quite the sight bent over Clover's leg, rewrapping the dressing.

"What do you think, Doc?" Cole said, hoping not to startle her. "She was favoring it the other day but today she seems better."

Lexi straightened upright, smoothing the back of her skirt. Her high ponytail accentuated her cheekbones. Shane was a fool to let her slip out of his fingers, but his cheating and shotgun wedding to a one-night stand back when they were eighteen tended to cost a man everything.

"She looks good." Lexi stepped gracefully from the stall, almost matching Cole's height in her heels. "I wanted to double-check on her. My patients can't tell me when something's wrong. I feel like I'm constantly playing detective."

"I figured you'd be up at the house, making wedding gowns out of toilet paper or whatever it is you women do when you get together."

"Do I look like the wedding gown type to you?" Lexi asked, spinning around. "Come on, who are we kidding?"

"If the gown was bloodred, I could see you walking down the aisle in it."

They both laughed at the thought, although Lexi admitted the idea had possibilities.

"I'm heading up there in a minute. I couldn't have a good time without checking in on Clover first."

"I've been wanting to talk to you about Billy Stevens." Cole stopped her before she left. "Is there any sort of equine veterinary assistant program you know of that he could be a part of?"

"I've noticed him hanging around quite a bit, but I didn't know if he was interested in the horses or if I had a fan." Lexi winked. "Let me see what I can do and I'll get back to you."

Cole thanked her and sought out his youngest brother. The number of grooms, wranglers and trainers required to run a ranch this size was mind-boggling. Chase had helped more with the breed management program this past year, but now with the new expansion, Cole felt he needed an extra set of hands. He supported his brothers continuing with their rodeoing, but with two-hundred-and-fifty thousand acres spread out over four counties, he'd be ecstatic the day they decided to call it quits. How his father had managed was beyond him. If he'd only given the man the credit he deserved back then instead of taking him for granted.

The thought had crossed his mind to talk to his brothers about promoting Nicolino to general operations manager, letting him oversee all the divisions so Cole could concentrate more of his energy on the breeding and hippotherapy programs. If there was one thing he was certain he and his brothers would agree on, it was Nicolino's capability to handle the job. The question remained, would he want the increased responsibility?

The sounds of female laughter filled the ranch. Cole knew one of the voices belonged to Tess and he stopped along the pathway to the ranch office to see if he could distinguish hers from the rest. Unable to do so, he closed his eyes, remembering how she'd looked when he proposed to her. He also remembered the look of disgust on her face when Shane burst through the door slinging mud before she had a chance to answer.

It did give him a chance to talk with Shane for a few minutes that afternoon before Shane announced Cole was going to have to hoof it back to the main house because—how did he put it?—jackasses walked behind horses, they didn't ride them. He rode away leaving Cole in a cloud of dust. The walk did nothing to ease his mind but it taught him one thing, his boots were not made for walking and he was in desperate need of new soles. He was grateful when one of the colt trainers drove up in a ranch Jeep and gave him a lift back to the stables.

Finding Chase in the ranch office, he reviewed some ideas for the combined equine academy with his brother, and once again, Cole called the contractors his father lined up for the job and asked them to hold off. They weren't happy, but upon hearing they would need to re-quote the project for a larger facility, they agreed to sit tight. Phoning the architect last, Cole arranged a meeting for the day after the wedding. That should give him enough time to pin Shane down.

"Do you have a moment?"

Tess stood in the doorway in a stunning cream-and-rose-colored dress. Her auburn hair was tousled loosely around her heart-shaped face, and her long, lean legs peeked out from under the voluminous skirt. Her glamorous bright red, movie-star lipstick caught his attention in more than one way.

"Wow." Cole trailed his gaze down the length of her body, to her cream-colored, wickedly high platform heels. "Wow."

"All right, one *wow* was enough—you sound like Bert. What is it with all these fancy bridal showers nowadays? In New York, everyone books a wild weekend getaway or they have some lavish affair followed by a night of club hopping. In the South, they go all out like it's high tea meets the Victoria's Secret catalog."

"Tess." Cole strode across the room and locked the office door. He blindly reached behind him and flipped the receiver off the base of the phone. Reaching into his pocket, he bent down on one knee once again and asked, "Will you do me the honor of being my wife and a mother to Ever?"

"Where on earth did you get a ring from?" Tess asked in surprise.

"I've had it for two years and I figured if I was going to ask you to marry me again, I was going to do it right this time, although the ranch office wasn't exactly what I had in mind."

"I don't know what to say."

"Yes would be a pretty good start!" Cole nervously laughed, sliding the antique ruby-and-diamond ring on her finger.

"Yes!" Tess cried. "I'll marry you."

Standing before her, he didn't know what to do with his hands anymore. Here she was dressed beautifully and he was covered in horse slobber and manure.

"I'm sorry, I'm filthy," Cole said. "I probably should have waited, but the moment seemed right and it's still early enough for you to call Avery and give her the news."

"Avery?" Tess seemed surprised to hear the woman's name mentioned. "Cole—"

Cole unlocked the door and handed her the phone. "You can call her from here. I'll be right back."

Running from the office to the main house, Cole pulled off his boots, hopping across the porch on one foot. Tearing off his shirt, he bounded up the main staircase. The wolf whistles that greeted him made him realize the bridal shower wasn't over with quite yet.

"Sorry, ladies," he called over his shoulder. "I have an engagement to celebrate."

"Jesse's?" he heard his mother ask.

"No, mine!" Cole slammed the bathroom door and

jumped in the shower to scrub away the dirt from the day. "Oh, no!" His eyes flew open, soap stinging them.

Jumping out of the shower, he quickly wrapped the towel around his waist.

"I can't believe I left her there like that! I could have at least escorted her to the house."

Starting down the stairs, he remembered his lack of clothes and ran back to the bedroom to throw on a pair of jeans and shirt. There was no time for his boxer briefs and in his haste he almost ruined his wedding night, considering his zipper nearly got the best of him.

Bounding back down the stairs, he realized the house was empty. Pulling his boots back on over his bare feet, he sprinted across the yard, vaulting the gate and racing to the ranch office, praying she didn't walk out on him again. Turning the corner, he was greeted with a *fine, how do you do* by his mother, followed by Maggie's chastising him for proposing then running off on her daughter. The sound of thirty-some-odd women congratulating him was almost enough to send him running back to the house until he felt a hand reach for his and pull him in the opposite direction.

"I called Avery," Tess shouted, over the madness. "She wants us to meet her at the office right away."

Hand in hand, they raced across the yard, Cole impressed with the way Tess managed to keep up even in heels. "When you live in the city and are constantly missing the bus, you learn to run in these things. Oh, crap, wait a minute."

Tess turned and shouted across the yard. "Miranda, I'm so sorry for stealing your thunder today."

Miranda threw her head back and laughed. "Don't give it a second thought. Go meet with your attorney and see what you can do about bringing that little girl home."

"Come on." Cole grabbed her hand and took off toward the car.

Cole thought he knew every one of Tess's expressions until he saw the way her face lit up when Avery informed them their chances of adopting Ever were much greater now.

"I've made arrangements with Ever's Child Protective Services caseworker and she'd like to meet with you and Ever tomorrow morning at Monkey Junction, if that works for you."

"Of course it works!" Tess beamed.

LATER THAT EVENING, Tess and Cole discussed the renovations they would need to kick into high gear on the cottage and were surprised when Shane offered to take the lead since he had already begun work on another one last year with their father. Not willing to question his motives, Cole and Tess accepted his offer.

The instant Cole's head hit the pillow that evening, the world around him faded to dreams of holding Tess in his arms while they both drifted off to sleep.

The following morning, Avery and both families piled into two of the ranch's black Lincoln Navigators and made their way to Monkey Junction. Not prepared for the ambush of relatives, CPS caseworker Fannie Mason clearly seemed taken aback by the large crowd that entered the facility's small front office.

"Quite the families you both have," Fannie said, closing the door to the office. "The old saying *it takes a village to raise a child* certainly holds true in this situation and I'm pleased to see such a strong support system in place."

"Normally we don't travel in packs." Cole sat rigidly on the edge of his chair. "I hope bringing everyone was all right."

"This isn't the normal adoption process, but I had the opportunity to work with Ms. Griffin once before and she's a risk taker." Fannie nodded to Avery. "I understand your family is Ever's benefactor and due to the previously established relationship I'm making some allowances. That's not to say we can skip any of the steps here. There are more prescreenings and the first thing we're going to do is run a background check, so we'll need to get you digitally fingerprinted tomorrow."

Tess slipped her hand into Cole's while Fannie continued to explain about the Adoption Education Seminar they needed to attend before they moved forward with the home study. Her pulse beat through her palm, matching his own nervousness.

"Since the house you intend on living in with Ever isn't available for a home study, we will need to conduct one on the main house where you've agreed to live for now and then another one when the renovations are completed."

Cole nodded and listened, thankful Avery and Tess took notes and asked the questions.

"Even though you may turn out to be the perfect family," Fannie stressed, "it's my job to insure you're the perfect family for Ever."

The questions seemed routine at first, asking about schools in their area, jobs and lifestyle. Although it was hard to see past the woman's neutral expression, Cole felt Fannie was impressed with the fact Ever would have a hippotherapy facility at her disposal.

After the preliminary questions, Ever joined them

and Fannie asked if she understood that Cole and Tess wanted to adopt her.

Instead of responding, Ever climbed down from her chair and, with the aid of her crutches, slowly walked toward Tess and Cole. Meeting her halfway, they knelt on the floor as Ever leaned into them, struggling to release her arms from the crutches so she could hug them.

"I think I have my answer on how she feels about you both." Fannie smiled.

"There's nothing we wouldn't do for her," Tess said over the top of Ever's head, her eyes filled with tears.

"Don't cry." Ever looked up at Tess. "It's going to be all right."

Cole admired the girl's willingness to comfort Tess and her ability to bring a smile to everyone's face in a matter of seconds.

"Ever needs to stay on schedule with all her regular therapies," Fannie continued, while Ever tucked herself between Tess and Cole on the small couch.

He listened to Fannie review Ever's current schedule. The universe was cruel when a child had to worry about her next doctor's appointment instead of thinking about what to dress her Barbie or the flavor of ice cream she wanted for dessert. At four years old, Ever had already dealt with more than most people did in a lifetime.

Ever sat back with her braced legs stretched out in front of her while she played with the drawstrings on her pink hoodie, her eyes heavy from boredom. Glancing down at Tess's notepad, Cole saw she wrote down every word Fannie said while Avery fired off questions regarding Ever's medical history. A part of him wanted to stand up and scream, *Just let us love Ever!*

Ever shifted and laid her head against Tess's arm.

Adjusting so Ever could lie down, Tess placed her pad on the floor and rested her hand on Ever's tiny shoulder. It was the most natural scene, Cole thought to himself, as if they already were a family.

After a few more questions, Fannie asked if they would leave the room so she could talk with Ever alone. After about twenty minutes, Fannie opened the door and Ever slowly made her way through. "Thank you, Ever." Fannie opened the door while Ever made her way out to the sidewalk alongside the corral fence. Nancy lifted a tired-looking Ever and carried her the rest of the way to her therapy horse. Poncho stood nearby and Ever wanted to stop and pet him first.

"Can we go talk to her?" Tess asked.

"Not right now." Fannie stepped aside. "I wanted to speak with you two a little more."

Tess and Cole filed in behind Avery, while Fannie closed the door and placed her notes on top of her briefcase.

"Is everything okay?" Cole anxiously tapped his thumb on the arm of the chair.

"This is a major adjustment for Ever, and I want you to be prepared for some mixed emotions." The caseworker removed her glasses and slowly looked from Tess to Cole. "From what I've seen and heard, I think you two will make fine parents for Ever and we will continue to move forward immediately."

"You mean we're approved?" Tess gripped Cole's arm.

"It means you've passed the first of many stages," Avery interjected. "But you're a lot closer than you were before."

"Once I receive your background check results and provide vaccination records for all of the animals Ever will come in contact with, we'll schedule the first of many supervised home visits. Oh, and one more thing, do you two have a wedding date set?"

"Not yet," Tess responded.

"They aren't planning a long engagement," Avery added. "I assure you they will be married long before the adoption is finalized."

Cole intertwined his fingers in Tess's, giving her a gentle squeeze. He knew Tess was happy but her body was rigid. A nervous smile formed on her lips when they rose to leave. Sensing that the stress of the morning was starting to wear her down, he pulled her close to him and wrapped her in his arms.

"I can't believe we've made it this far," she whispered, sobbing softly. "We actually have a chance of being a family."

"More than a chance." Cole lifted her chin and kissed her lightly. "We'll bring Ever home soon."

Chapter Eleven

Once they were back at the ranch, Tess excused herself and walked around the grounds, trying to wrap her head around the idea that Bridle Dance would soon become her home.

Seeing Chase near the stables, she asked if he'd saddle one of the horses for her.

"Here you go," he said, leading a colorful white-and-brown paint gelding. "This is Howard."

"Howard?" Tess furrowed her brows. "Howard the horse? That's original."

"Dad rescued quite a few horses in his day." Chase ran his hand down the horse's mane. "He won't give you any trouble, but are you sure you don't want someone to accompany you? It's been years since you've ridden."

"Chase Langtry." Tess snatched the reins from him. "I had riding trophies under my belt before you learned to walk. I think I can manage old Howard here."

Chase was ready to argue with her when Cole stepped in and offered to go with her, telling the groom to saddle Blackjack.

"We haven't had a moment alone," Cole said. "Are you all right with this?"

"Of course." Tess hopped twice in the stirrup and

swung her right leg up and over the horse's back, immediately regretting wearing jeans with a very small amount of give to them. "Today was a little overwhelming with everyone there. Growing up, there were only three of us, four if you counted Bert on holidays. I'm not used to the noise or this many people involved in my personal life, but it's a good thing. I kind of enjoyed it."

"We're a boisterous bunch." Cole climbed into the saddle when the groom returned. "For the record, I had no idea they were going with us."

"It's all right." Tess lightly nudged her horse forward with her lower legs. "No one can say we don't have a great support system."

She inhaled and let out a slow breath. Her trip home was supposed to provide some much needed downtime away from things in New York. She certainly hadn't anticipated switching her single, city-girl status for that of a small-town married mother. Excited and scared out of her wits, Tess looked forward to the future.

When Cole kissed her in the gas station parking lot during their first trip to Monkey Junction, she knew what she'd been afraid to admit two years ago in Vegas. She'd loved him then, and she loved him now. Cole's proposal was sweet and touching, but Tess feared it was more about Ever and she couldn't help but feel a little disappointed.

Twenty-four hours ago, she was attending Miranda's bridal shower. The more time she spent with the woman, the more she understood why everyone liked her. She was spunky, sassy and definitely held her own when it came to Jesse. They were a perfect match and anyone could see the chemistry between them. But did the same chemistry exist between Cole and her or were they only together for Ever? Tess almost felt cheated in a way.

"Hello?" Cole said. Tess looked over her shoulder to see him talking on his phone. "Okay, tomorrow's fine. We look forward to it."

Cole cantered up beside Tess. "That was Fannie. She said Nancy felt Ever was shortchanged out of most of her session today since our meeting with her ran long. She asked if we wanted to meet at Monkey Junction tomorrow afternoon and be a part of her therapy. Alone. I said we would."

"I wonder what she means by *be a part of it.*"

"We'll find out soon enough." Cole reached out and tugged on Tess's denim jacket. "Is there anyplace you want to ride to?"

"I'd love to go back to the cottage."

Tess followed Cole down a narrow dirt trail, her saddle creaking beneath her. Howard's ears twitched at the birds chirping invisibly in the brush on either side of them. Leaning forward, Tess patted the horse on the side of the neck. Howard nickered, nodding his head in approval.

A clearing came into view. *Their cottage.* Cole tied Blackjack to the hitching post built into the front of the porch, and held Howard's bridle for Tess when she dismounted.

"Has someone been here?" Tess stepped up on the porch. "I don't remember it looking so tidy."

Without a word, Cole held the door open for her and Tess entered the house. Reaching for the switch, Cole flicked the overhead lights on, allowing Tess to truly see the room for the first time.

"I had the power turned on this morning. The place needs a lot of work, but it has potential." Cole ran his hands over the plaster and lath walls. "See how thick these are? Underneath this are the original timbers used to build the house. I'd love to restore it to its former glory. With your approval, of course."

"My approval." Tess laughed. "This is your land, Cole. You don't need my approval on anything."

Cole tugged Tess into his arms. "That's where you're wrong, Tess." Leaning in close, he took her lips softly. She relented for a moment, before pulling back. "I promise there won't be any interruption tonight."

Tilting her head in slight confusion, she followed the direction of Cole's gaze to the kitchen counter, where a picnic basket and a bouquet of flowers waited for them.

Tess opened the basket to reveal a bottle of chilled champagne, assorted cheeses and fruits.

"How were you able to prepare this when you didn't even know I was heading out for a ride?" Tess asked. "And the champagne's even cold!"

"The beauty of text messaging, my dear." Cole removed the flutes from the basket and placed them on the counter. "I sent Nicolino a message when you were ahead of me. He and my mother raided the leftovers from the shower and they drove up here with everything. I figured you would have suspected something when we went out of the way around that copse of trees. I needed to buy some time so we'd have our own *quiet* moment to celebrate."

Removing the foil wrapper and wire cage from the bottle of Perrier-Jouët champagne, Cole sent the cork soaring toward the ceiling with his thumbs. Handing Tess her glass, he raised his own.

"Our first toast in our house." Cole winked at her. "Here's to new beginnings and a happy *Ever* after."

Tess allowed herself to enjoy this moment alone with Cole in *their* house. With the better lighting, she easily envisioned how the furniture would flow from one room to the next. Setting her glass on the counter, she took Cole's and placed it next to hers. Wrapping her arms around the man willing to give her the world in exchange for giving a child she adored a home, Tess met his lips with a passion and fervor that was second only to the other night in the front seat of his truck. Grabbing the blanket Nicolino thoughtfully left next to the picnic basket, Cole didn't waste a second spreading it out on the floor.

Clothes fell away along with the walls that surrounded both of their hearts. For the moment, Tess didn't need to hear the words *I love you*. With each stroke of his hand, every touch of his lips against her flesh, she felt how much she meant to him. And for now, that's all she needed.

THEY RODE BACK to the main house shortly after sunset. Slightly disheveled and giggling, they were surprised to see Jesse, Miranda and Kay staring at them from the kitchen table.

"What are you two doing here?" Cole tried in vain to tuck his shirt in.

"Reviewing the wedding plans with Mom." Jesse laughed. "I don't have to ask what you two were doing."

Miranda snickered while Kay swatted at them both. "It wasn't too long ago you two were sneaking off for a little one-on-one time."

"Here's to the honeymoon never being over." Miranda raised her coffee mug.

After seeing Tess home for the night, Cole found his mother bustling about the kitchen.

"Another wedding to plan." Kay shook her head. "Leave it to my children to get married back-to-back."

"Relax, Mom." Cole enjoyed watching the lines of

frustration in his mother's forehead when she fretted over small things. "Tess isn't the big-formal-wedding type. Who knows, maybe we'll fly to Hawaii for a weekend ceremony. How would that be?"

"Your father loved Hawaii." Kay lowered herself onto one of the kitchen island stools. "I remember when we stepped off that little plane in Maui and those beautiful Hawaiian girls placed a lei over his head, why, he felt like royalty."

Cole hadn't thought much more past what happened this afternoon in the kitchen of the cottage, but the moment Hawaii came out of his mouth, he loved the idea.

Wanting to run it past Maggie first, Cole thought it would be a wonderful surprise if he planned a Hawaiian wedding with their immediate families present. Tess wouldn't realize where they were going until they reached the Big Island. That was Tess's type of wedding. Pomp and circumstance could be fun, but it wasn't Tess.

Excited, he dialed Maggie's cell phone, hoping she'd be in favor of the idea. Overjoyed was more like it. She said she would drop a few well-placed questions to make certain Tess didn't want a traditional wedding.

The following morning, Tess was at the ranch working with Kay on some marketing ideas. Frustrated he still hadn't pinned down Shane, Cole drove into town hoping to spot his brother's truck at the house of one of his many girlfriends.

Coming up empty, Cole swung into Hanson's Hardware to see if the locks he'd ordered to replace the rusted ones on the outer perimeter gates had come in. Slappy Hanson animatedly discussed the work they were doing on the cottage.

"How did you know about that?" Cole asked, though

he shouldn't be surprised at how fast word traveled. Still, he didn't think anyone other than the family knew.

"Shane was in here first thing this morning picking up a few things. Said he already had a crew lined up to work on the place."

When Shane offered to renovate the cottage, Cole hadn't expected him to jump in feetfirst. Driving past the main house on the dirt road that traversed Bridle Dance, Cole found himself behind a trailer carrying a construction Dumpster.

Stopping in front of the cottage, he watched Shane direct the driver where to set his load. Slappy wasn't kidding. Shane had multiple crews working on every inch of the house. As he parked the Jeep alongside Shane's ranch rig, the sounds of a pressure washer startled Cole. He glanced over to see it being used to remove layers of dirt from the outside of the cottage.

"Cole." Shane waved to him. "You have to see what we found under the plaster and lath."

The inside of the house contained more people than were outside. Chunks of plaster were already stripped from the wall, revealing smooth Western red cedar logs.

"The logs are almost untouched, except where the lath was nailed into it, but we can repair that and no one will be the wiser," Shane said enthusiastically. "I called in a few favors down at the building department and obtained the permits. I know you don't like it when I throw the Langtry weight around, but this time, I didn't think you'd mind."

"Where's this coming from, Shane?" Cole asked, confused by his brother's sudden change of heart.

"I figured I owed you for the past few months." Shane slapped his brother on the shoulder.

Cole held his hand out. "Truce?"

"Truce." Shane shook, pulling Cole into one of those male half hug, half pat on the back deals.

"So why aren't you planning out your half of the facility?" Cole asked, still curious to know what had driven his brother to take on renovating his house at warp speed.

"I saw how much this meant to you and Tess when we met with the caseworker. Fannie, was it? Anyway, when Fannie stressed the home study, I thought it was crazy to hold up the adoption because of the cottage and having to do two inspections, so I figured if they can build a house from scratch in a week on that *Extreme Makeover* show, we can renovate one by the time our background checks clear. Speaking of which, aren't you and Tess scheduled for eleven this morning?"

Cole checked his watch. He needed to hustle so he could pick Tess up and make their digital fingerprint appointment. Afterward, they would head over to Monkey Junction and see the precious soon-to-be addition to their family. He would be thrilled when the day came to bring Ever home with them.

"WELL, THAT WASN'T what I expected," Tess said, when they left the fingerprinting location. "A scanner I can handle, not like those treat-you-like-a-criminal, black-ink cards. Remember when they fingerprinted us in kindergarten and how scared we were thinking we were being arrested? It was one way to get us to behave for the rest of the year."

"I'd forgotten that." Cole smiled at the memory. "You thought they were going to lock us up and throw books at us."

Tess tossed her head back and laughed. "How was

I supposed to know what that stupid phrase meant? I was five."

Arriving at Monkey Junction a little early, they decided to grab a cup of coffee at Starbucks on the other side of the highway. From their seat in the café, they'd be able to see Lorraine's minivan turn in the parking lot.

"Do you find it odd that Ever's foster mother won't speak to us?" Tess asked.

"We've spoken." Cole thought back to the few conversations he'd had with the woman. "She's not around very often, just long enough to drop Ever off and pick her up. I honestly figured she was running errands while Ever was in therapy, although I thought it would be nice if she'd stayed and cheered her on. She had a much better rapport with my father."

"Why's that?" Tess asked.

"Lorraine is supposed to notify us if Ever needs anything at any given moment, regardless of the time of day or night. There have been a few instances when I found out from Eileen that Ever was stuck in the state's red tape because Lorraine didn't want to *burden* me."

"Was that what was going on the first day I met Ever? You seemed put out that Lorraine didn't call and tell you Ever was walking."

"It was a big deal for her to be able to walk on her own." Cole still felt upset. "I know I have no legal right to it, but sharing in the good news would have been nice."

"Do you think there is something else going on there?" Tess asked.

"I've wondered if she's doing this for the money and she's afraid of how much she'll lose once we take Ever away from her. Or she really wants to adopt Ever herself but can't afford to. Either way, we're a threat to her."

"Which do you think it is?"

"Honestly, I think it's the latter of the two. Eileen and Nancy both speak highly of Lorraine, but she avoids me like the plague. She wears a wedding ring but I haven't met her husband. Ever doesn't say anything bad about her, not that I've spoken to her much about Lorraine. I don't know. I have no right to judge considering it appears she's taken good care of Ever for the past four years."

"I didn't stop to really think that we're taking her away from people she might love." Tess's eyes immediately filled with tears. "I assumed she'd want to come live with us."

Cole handed her a napkin, wrapping his arm around her shoulders.

"I know," he whispered against her hair. The same thoughts had passed through his own mind. "It won't be easy taking her from the one family she's known, but you have to remind yourself, in the end, our adopting Ever will give her peace of mind and stability. Without adoption, she can be removed from that family at any time and placed in a care facility."

"I know." Tess wiped at her eyes. "I'm assuming some sort of psychological counseling is covered in those training classes Fannie mentioned."

Cole nodded. He couldn't fathom the terror Ever must feel at the thought of being removed from her foster family and sent to live with him and Tess. He believed they were doing the right thing, but a part of him wondered if maybe leaving her where she was and helping Lorraine and her family adopt Ever would be best. Being a parent was no easy task if decisions like these needed to be made on a daily basis.

Tess placed her hand on top of his, as if reading his

mind, and offered a half smile. Deciding it was close enough to Ever's hippotherapy appointment, they drove across the street to Monkey Junction. An hour passed and Ever still didn't appear. Both Cole and Eileen tried to reach Lorraine, but she wasn't answering either her house or mobile phone.

Another hour ticked by and Tess placed countless calls to Fannie, leaving messages. Cole called Kay and asked if she'd heard anything. Fearing the worst, Tess began to call the local hospitals, when Eileen emerged from the office, looking grim.

Tess reached for Cole's hand, squeezing hard.

"That was Lorraine," Eileen began. "Ever had a seizure last night and is in the hospital for testing."

"I told her to call me if anything happened to Ever!" Cole raged. "Did she say what hospital?"

Tess frantically dialed her mother, explaining what they knew of the situation. Maggie promised to tell the rest of the family, urging them both to remain calm and positive.

"I'm worried, Cole," Tess said, on the way to the hospital.

"I know you are, sweetie." Cole reached for Tess over the Jeep's gearshift.

"But she had a seizure," Tess said softly.

After signing in and locating Ever's floor, they went up to her room. Fannie greeted them outside.

"How is she?" Cole asked breathlessly.

"I spoke briefly with the nurses when I arrived," Fannie began. "Ever's stable and only had the one seizure. They've been running tests to determine what the cause may have been, but so far nothing's been conclusive."

"I guess that's good news," Cole said, hoping they

wouldn't find anything seriously wrong. "Is she allowed visitors?"

"Cole, Tess, I want to talk to you before you go in." Fannie directed them to chairs in the waiting area and took a seat facing them. "I want to talk for a little bit and remind you that even with mild cerebral palsy, there is still a possibility Ever will have other problems throughout her life. You need to be one hundred percent certain when it comes to adopting a child whose medical requirements may change at any given moment."

"We understand that." Cole felt his frustration begin to mount.

"Tess?" Fannie placed a hand on her shoulder. "You're not saying anything. Are you all right with this?"

Slowly lifting her head, Tess looked from Fannie to Cole. "I'm not going to lie to you." Tess tucked a lock of hair behind her ear. "A seizure is serious whether it recurs or not. It's unexpected, but I understand that doctors and hospitals are a part of all parenting. What concerns me is what this means for Ever."

"That's a normal reaction and I wouldn't blame you if you said you were scared." Fannie leaned forward in her chair. "When you go in, Ever's needs come before your own. Adoption isn't an easy decision and one I don't want you to take lightly, but you must be able to come to terms with the reality of ongoing care. If you can't do that, then please let me know. She's already been through enough."

"What do you mean she's been through enough already?" Cole questioned. "She can't possibly remember being given up for adoption."

"Lorraine and her husband have fostered many children over the years, some with disabilities, and some without. Ever's been with them the longest, and a little over a year ago, they decided to adopt her."

"You were right." Tess looked at Cole. "We knew there was a reason Lorraine was never around when we were. Does this mean she'll challenge our adopting Ever?"

"Lorraine's situation is unique," Fannie continued. "Already a part of the system, she and her husband Guthrie were approved to adopt Ever and were well on their way to completing their six-month supervisory period when Guthrie was killed by a drunk driver. We asked Lorraine if she needed respite care or if having Tess was too much for her to handle while she dealt with her husband's death, but she remained strong and didn't let it affect Ever. When she still wanted to move forward with the adoption, she had to complete a single-parent-home study and reset her supervisory period from the beginning."

"Is that where she's at today?" Cole felt Tess's hand tighten in his at the question. "In the middle of her supervisory period? Why wasn't anyone in my family notified of this before?"

"Because as her benefactor, it was none of your business," Fannie said matter-of-factly. "You provide her care, Cole, but that doesn't give you any other rights. Guthrie died before your father became involved, and discussing it after the fact was pointless. Lorraine has done remarkably well with Ever, better than anyone expected, and we're very thankful for her efforts. She's gone above and beyond in some extremely trying times."

"Where does that leave her?" Tess solemnly asked. "I don't want to be responsible for tearing Ever away from the one mother she knows."

"For reasons I am not at liberty to discuss, Lorraine feels Ever would be better in a household with a mother and father." Fannie directed her attention to Cole. "Lorraine doesn't have a problem with you or your family. She was very grateful to your father, but at that time, she was still planning on adopting Ever herself. Relinquishing her will be very emotional for Lorraine."

"Then why is she doing it?" Tess asked.

"I can't discuss that with you." Fannie sighed. "Lorraine feels Ever would be better off with you and Cole, but that doesn't mean she wants to stand around and watch it happen. I can try to arrange a meeting between you and Lorraine. I can't guarantee she'll agree to it, though."

"I think we'd be more comfortable sitting down and hearing where she's coming from," Tess said.

"I'll see what I can do." Fannie walked them toward the nurse's station. "This is Tess Dalton and Cole Langtry. I added them to Ever's visitor-approved list earlier. May they go in and see her now?"

Cole placed his hand on the small of Tess's back as they entered Ever's room. Their tiny princess lay motionless on a hospital bed ten times her size. Tess turned into Cole's chest and stifled a sob. Gently rubbing her between her shoulders, he felt her take a deep breath and compose herself.

Facing Ever, Tess walked slowly to the bed. Along the wall, machines with black screens and machines with green screens beeped and took readings. An oxygen tube wrapped around her tiny ears and fed into her nose. Another monitor was taped to her finger, a cuff strapped to her arm. Cole had to force himself not to cry.

"She looks so fragile," Tess whispered.

Bars framed the bed so Ever wouldn't tumble out. Pulling a stool up to either side of her bed, Tess and Cole reached through the bars to hold Ever's hands.

"I've never felt so helpless." Tess brushed aside Ever's hair with her free hand. "She has sensors stuck all over her body. She doesn't even look real."

"She's a strong girl." Cole wanted to reassure himself as much as Tess. "I'm sorry." A nurse entered the room. "We're going to take Miss Ever down for some testing now, but you can come back tomorrow."

"Tomorrow?" Cole wiped at his eyes. "We can't see her later today?"

"Visiting hours are only until four in the pediatric wing." The nurse looked sympathetic. "Do we have your number at the desk? We can call you if there's any change in her condition."

"Why isn't she awake?" Tess asked. "She hasn't moved once."

"It's the medication they gave her earlier to keep her sedated. Please don't worry, so far everything looks good."

Tess stared out the window, occasionally dabbing at her eyes and face during their silent drive home. The sun had long since set, enveloping the car in darkness when he parked in front of the Daltons' house.

Tess made no move to leave. Propping her arm on the windowsill, she slowly ran her finger down the passenger-side window.

"How could we not know about her foster family?" Tess asked quietly.

"Maybe my father knew but I never asked. The few conversations I had with Lorraine were about Ever's financial needs, not their home life. At the time, more would have felt like an invasion of privacy." Cole felt he had been kept in the dark the entire time. "Fannie said it wasn't our business, but I still feel like we should have known."

"That's it?" Tess asked.

"That's what?"

"That's how you're going to neatly sum up why we don't know more about the little girl we plan on adopting?"

"I don't understand, Tess, what are you trying to say?"

"So what if Fannie didn't tell us about Ever's foster father? We didn't know because we never took the time to find out."

"We can't change the past, Tess. All we can do is more forward and learn from our mistakes, while hoping we don't make new ones."

"I need some time." Tess pulled her jacket tighter across her chest.

"What?" Cole asked, hoping he'd heard wrong.

"I need some time to absorb all of this. I'm not walking away from you or anything, I just need some time to work through this. I'll call you if I hear anything and please do the same for me."

He watched her step down from the Jeep and into the house. The guttural groan that followed no longer belonged to Cole, but to the man longing for the little girl alone in a hospital bed ninety miles away from him. A man who wanted to hold that child close and take away her fears. And do the same for the woman he feared had just walked out of his life for a second time.

Chapter Twelve

"Cole!" Kay flew to him when he entered the house. "Why haven't you called us? How is Ever?"

"She's stable." Cole sat down at the kitchen table. "No one knows anything until they run more tests, but as of two hours ago, she was hanging in there."

Cole's family was gathered around the table and he explained the little bit Fannie had told them about Ever's seizure. He also spoke about Lorraine's husband. Ever's foster mother hadn't been in the waiting room or the hallway, but he hoped she would be there at some point to offer the little girl comfort.

He hated that he'd thought the worst of the woman all along, but if she'd told them what was going on, they would have supported her. It would have been nice to at least have a conversation with her so they understood where the other was coming from.

"Did Tess say anything else before she left?" Miranda asked.

"That was it, she wanted some time." Cole braced his hands on his knees. "What does that even mean?"

"I can understand if she's feeling a little crowded." His mother stood before him. "This is a huge, life-changing responsibility."

"One I'm ready for." Cole twisted off the top of the water bottle she handed him and tossed it into the trash. "I've never been more certain of anything in my life. It was horrible seeing Ever tied to all those machines."

"Welcome to parenthood, son."

When the house cleared out Kay joined Cole on the leather sofa in front of the fireplace. The warm glow and snapping of the sap from the oak that burned within its brick depths did nothing to ease his mind.

Wordlessly, Cole cursed being in a toasty house, with his mother by his side. He pictured Ever alone in a strange place and a cold, stark room. His heart broke in ways he didn't think possible. One way or another he was bringing Ever home to stay and he didn't care if he had to spend his last dollar to do it.

"Don't get mad at me for asking this, honey." His mother's soft voice cut through his thoughts. "Can you honestly deny having any doubts about your ability to care for and deal with Ever's medical needs?"

Cole leaned his head against the couch and squeezed his eyes shut.

"I'll take your silence as a no." Kay laid her hand over Cole's. "You're human and it's okay to have doubts. Tess was honest and up front with you, which is more than you can say for yourself."

Of course he had doubts about Ever's medical needs, but her happiness far outweighed any risks and doubts out there, and whatever problems arose, he would deal with them. Wasn't that what parents did? They supported and comforted their children, no matter the hour or the situation. You squelched that fear and remained strong for your kids.

"Tess can't just walk away and avoid the situation," Cole said. "Not at this stage."

"Sure she can, honey, especially if she's scared." Kay tucked her legs underneath her, reclining into the corner of the couch. "She hasn't left either one of you. She's just looking for a little time to think things through. I can't tell you how many times I was scared when you boys were growing up. One of you was always in the hospital with broken bones, appendicitis, concussions. You four had me downright terrified sometimes."

"If you were scared you never showed it," Cole said.

"Not to you or your brothers." Kay reached out, resting her hand upon his shoulder. "Your father saw my fear and I saw his. We relied on each other and were there for one another to get through it, together."

"Fine," Cole agreed. "I'll give her all the time she needs."

"When you give birth to a child, you have nine months to prepare for the little tyke," Kay said. "Then you ease into the day-to-day routine, learning as you go along. Adopting a four-year-old is altogether different. Suddenly you have a walking, talking, active child and there is no easing into anything. One day she's not in your life, the next you have a little person asking you why the sky's blue."

"I hadn't looked at it like that."

"You have a big heart. Probably the biggest of any of you boys, and I don't think your brothers would argue with me on it, either. Adopting a child is not easy and it's a huge adjustment for the parents and the child, but in the end, I think that's what Tess was trying to get you to understand. She didn't tell you to leave and not to come back."

"No, she didn't."

"When you do talk to Tess, you need to tell her your fears and concerns so she doesn't feel like she's the bad one. A successful marriage is one with open dialogue and communication."

Why was it mothers were always right? He would give Tess her space and he'd allow himself the same courtesy. Tomorrow's only saving grace was Jesse's bachelor trip.

TESS STOOD AT the edge of the street and watched Cole pull away.

"Tess," Maggie called from the porch. "Is that you, honey?"

Inhaling deeply, Tess plodded up the driveway and porch stairs.

"Tess, what's wrong?" Maggie wrapped her arm around her daughter, guiding her through the door. "Henry, where are you?"

Tess told her parents about the past few hours, and then swung her legs up and laid her head against the arm of the couch. Ricky jumped on her lap and made his way up her chest, lying across her, purring loudly while she stroked his back. The last thing she remembered was her mother covering her legs with a blanket.

Tess awoke shortly after midnight, Ricky asleep soundlessly on top of her. She reached into her pocket for her phone, waking her feline companion. One missed call. Disappointed to see it was from Treena Abbott, the headhunter in Austin she'd spoken to a few weeks earlier, she listened to the voice mail message. A company was interested in setting up an interview with her.

The salary of a large firm was tempting, but the commute no longer fit into her anticipated lifestyle. She sent Treena a polite email to thank her, and, scooping Ricky up in her arms, she climbed the stairs and slid beneath the covers of her bed. Normally her cat wasn't this attentive, but sensing her anguish, he stayed curled up on her pillow all night.

The next morning, Tess awoke with the overwhelming need to see Ever. She knew she could handle whatever came their way, even if she had to do it alone. Last night she told Cole she wasn't walking away from him, but damned if it didn't feel like a break-up when Tess told him she needed some time.

The thought of adopting Ever without Cole was her plan from the beginning. Once he became a part of it, it began to flow naturally as though they were really a family, fitting together seamlessly. Now Tess had difficulty imagining going through this alone and it bothered her beyond reason.

She quickly dressed and made her way to the hospital. The elevator doors opened and Tess saw a doctor leaving Ever's room.

"Excuse me, Doctor." Tess raced to catch up with him. "I'm Tess Dalton. Ever's CPS caseworker added me to her approved list. Have you found out why she had the seizure?"

"It's a pleasure, Ms. Dalton. I'm Dr. Sutter and it appears the seizure was a result of one of her new medications. It was an extremely rare side effect that only two patients exhibited in the case study. We're going to keep her here for observation for a few more days to be on the safe side. I expect Ever to be back to her usual self in no time."

"Thank you." Tess enthusiastically shook his hand. "I am so relieved."

"Tess?" a voice called from the waiting area. Lorraine stood in the middle of the room, looking forlorn.

"Lorraine." Tess walked over to the woman, who appeared thinner and paler than she had at Monkey Junction. "It's nice to finally meet you."

"Fannie said you wanted to talk to me."

"I do." Tess attempted to meet Lorraine's eyes, but she stared at the floor. Tess felt like the wicked witch, trying to steal away the little girl this woman had raised from infancy. "Can we grab a cup of coffee downstairs?"

Lorraine nodded and they rode the elevator in silence. Tess sat across from Lorraine in the cafeteria and debated how to start the conversation. She had a million questions but none of them seemed right to ask first.

"Fannie told us yesterday about your husband. I'm very sorry you had to go through that."

Lorraine lifted her head, her eyes filled with tears. "We really wanted to adopt her."

Tess's reached across the table and took Lorraine's hands in hers. The two women held each other's gaze, and instantly Tess understood why the woman had been so distant.

"Then why don't you?" Tess asked.

"Because after Guthrie died, I knew I couldn't give Ever the care she needed." Lorraine attempted a tight smile. "At least not like you and Cole can. She deserves a complete family, one who can provide more for her than I can."

"I'm so sorry." Tess looked down at the table. "I never meant to come in and take her from you."

Lorraine squeezed her hands. "Don't be sorry for me. You and Cole have so much more to offer her. I'm still dealing with the loss of my husband. Just promise me—promise me you'll take care of that little girl. I've loved her as if she were my own."

"I promise." Tess squeezed Lorraine's hand. "I promise she will always know who you are."

Not wanting your typical bachelor party, Jesse asked his brothers to join him and take their father's 1938 one-of-a-kind wooden twin-engine Chris-Craft Sportsman boat to Callicoon Lake. The overnight trip was to honor their father on the lake where they'd spent so many weekends camping and fishing when they were kids.

Leaving at four in the morning to make the three-hour drive, they launched the boat and visited each of the fishing coves their father loved. Chase pointed out where he had his first kiss and they laughed about the time Shane was bit by a pickerel and had to have his big toe stitched up.

At last they sat down in front of the fire they'd made to cook their catch. "I owe Tess an apology." Shane handed Cole another beer. "I wish Dad had come up with the combined facility idea so we didn't feel so left out of his plans. He was an all-or-nothing man, wasn't he?"

"That he was." Chase threw another battered catfish on the sizzling cast-iron pan.

"I'm getting married," Jesse sang, with a shot of whiskey in hand. "*M-A-R-R-I-E-D*. To the most beautiful woman in the world. Here I thought I was destined to be a bachelor."

"I'll have some of whatever he's drinking." Chase laughed.

Cole wanted to join in their celebration, but he found it increasingly difficult to think of anyone other than Ever. The following morning, Cole started cleaning up the campsite before dawn. By the time his brothers awoke, he had the truck packed and ready to hit the road.

"Do any of you mind if we take a slight detour on the way home?"

Parking the truck and boat across the back of the hospital parking lot a couple of hours later, the four men made their way to Ever's hospital room.

"You go on in, we'll wait for you out here," Shane said.

Pushing the door open, Cole saw Ever curled up on her bed. Ducking back out the door, he asked the station nurse where the gift shop was and purchased the softest and most huggable mahogany-colored teddy bear. All children deserved a teddy bear to hold on to, and once he was upstairs again, he had an idea. He told his brothers to insure every child in the hospital had their own stuffed animal to comfort them. And if the gift shop didn't have enough to go around, they should call the closest toy store to have them delivered.

As he approached her bedside, Ever opened her eyes and held her arms out to him.

"CC!" she cried out. "Please take me home, CC. Please."

Cole wrapped her in his arms as best the wires and sensors connected to her would allow. He wordlessly cursed the machines monitoring her, wanting to whisk her away to someplace warm and safe, where nothing could harm her.

Fighting the urge to take her and run, he squeezed the teddy bear between them.

"This is for you, honey."

Ever wrapped her small arms around the bear, still remaining close to him. He felt her fear in the slight tremble of her body. Her eyes were squeezed tight and he wondered if she were trying to will herself somewhere else.

He stayed with her until she fell asleep and the nurse came in to tell him morning visiting hours were over. Outside in the waiting area, his brothers sat with a very rosy-cheeked Fannie.

"Cole." A flustered Fannie jumped to her feet and shook his hand. "Your brothers are quite, um, entertaining."

Cole knew they made a formidable-looking crew. Not lacking in the looks department, they tended to draw attention when they were together, especially when they competed in the rodeo.

"I'm glad you're here," Cole said to the caseworker. "It saves me a phone call. I want to go ahead with the adoption."

"Have you spoken with Tess?" Fannie questioned.

"No, he hasn't," Jesse chimed in from his chair.

Cole rolled his eyes, "Not since the other day—she needed time."

"I think you should talk to Tess, too," Fannie said.

"We think you should, too," Chase added.

"What is this, a conspiracy?" Cole looked from Fannie to his brothers. "Don't tell me they got to you. I thought you were trained to be immune to bull—"

"I assure you your brothers did not *get to me.* But I am advising you to discuss your plans with Miss Dalton. In the meantime, I will move forward with the paperwork. You know I can't do much without your background-check results, which I've been told should be another day or so. Seems you know some people in high places."

After being reassured she would call Cole if anything changed with Ever, the four brothers left the hospital. Not wanting to discuss Tess, they talked strategies for the new equine facility. Cole, Jesse and Kay would run Dance of Hope and Shane and Chase would have their Ride 'em High! Rodeo School.

Chapter Thirteen

The sun was barely on the horizon when the Magpie crew drove under Double Trouble's iron arch, decorated heavily with white flowers and green ivy. The former Carter estate had had new life breathed into it since Miranda Archer came to town earlier that year after winning the Maryland lottery.

White satin ribbons and tulle wrapped around every tree and fence post. The horses in the pastures wore white bridles with pansies woven throughout their manes. Large white tents were set up in the south field, where the annual Fourth of July picnic took place.

"Bert, here are the keys." Maggie held out her hand. "Can you and Bridgett take the van back to the Magpie and reload by yourselves or do you need me to grab some of the waitstaff to help you?"

"We have it," Bert said. "Relax, Maggie. This isn't your first wedding, everything will be fine."

"You better knock on wood when you say that," Maggie called after him. He responded by knocking on Bridgett's head.

"You outdid yourself." Kay joined her best friend. "Miranda fell in love with the idea of these miniature pies. A few bites is all you need of a great pie."

"She wanted a dessert table and we gave her one. They're apple, cherry and pear and if they set the lighting up the way I asked them to, the sugar-coated crusts will sparkle."

A white runner with yellow rose petals divided the five rows of white wooden folding chairs into two large half circles on either side of the arbor. Each half circle would seat one hundred and fifty guests, Tess noted, taken aback by the unconventional yet gorgeous flow of the venue.

"Who designed the seating?" Tess asked "I've never seen that before."

"Miranda was worried that Jesse's side would have all the guests." Kay lowered her voice. "With being new in town and not having any family, we went with the circle instead. No matter where you sit, you have a view of the couple during the ceremony."

Placed on each seat was a tulle bag with birdseed for the guest to throw when the bride and groom walked down the aisle. Three hundred bags and Tess still had birdseed left over.

I hope everyone wants suet balls for Christmas.

Her mother's Best of Both Worlds wedding cake drew the most attention. Five layers regally stood upon an ornate sterling-silver platform, on loan from Kay. A traditional white wedding cake featured ornate scallop-and-pearl piping on one side and milk-chocolate fondant and dark fudge drizzles on the other, the chocolate flowing from tier to tier.

Jesse didn't look even the slightest bit nervous while he waited for Miranda to walk down the aisle. Cole served as his best man and it was nice seeing all four brothers stand together without looking like they wanted to kill each other.

Tess tensed when Cole turned in her direction. She hadn't spoken to him since the other day and appreciated the time he was giving her to think things over. But after Lorraine's declaration Tess felt Cole needed to know the truth.

Vicki, the maid of honor, and her bridesmaids, Lexi and Bridgett, made their way down the aisle in sage chiffon beaded empire-waist gowns. When the wedding march began everyone rose as Miranda walked down the aisle on Jon's arm in a strapless Yumi Katsura haute couture gown Tess would have deemed only appropriate for an extravagant wedding at the Plaza on Fifth Avenue in Manhattan. The tiers of silk-satin hemmed organza beneath a bodice embellished with delicately jeweled Swarovski crystals appeared right at home in the ranch setting.

Miranda's long blond hair was curled in ringlets and pinned back, forming a cascade of curls down her back. Carrying a simple white calla lily bouquet tied with a green satin ribbon, she made a stunning bride.

"Miranda," Mable began. "The day I first laid eyes on you, I knew you were a match for this here stubborn mule of a man. It is an honor to be a part of your lives, and to officiate over this wedding in front of our friends and family. Lordy, I sure hope this internet ordainment is legal."

Inside the wedding tents, plain white linen and china framed by ornate silver flatware covered the long tables. Tall cylindrical glass vases with two pure white hydrangeas each ran down the center of each table, with three smaller vases containing white votive candles between the arrangements.

Vicki had designed two wine racks that stood on the gift table next to a small stack of paper and twine. Each rack held five empty wine bottles in various shades. The bottles in the first rack were labeled one through four, for the next four years, with the extra bottle labeled with today's date. The bottles on the second rack were labeled in increments of five and guests wrote notes, tied them with the twine and slipped them inside the bottles.

Tonight the bride and groom would read the notes from the wedding day bottle and then on subsequent anniversaries would enjoy the many good wishes and blessings offered by their guests. It was a lovely gesture, one she would welcome at her own wedding.

Tess stared down at her vacant ring finger. She'd removed Cole's ring the other night, thinking it wasn't fair to keep leading him on if she was uncertain about their future together. She wished she had worn it today, though, because she did want to marry him.

Seeing Cole nearby, Tess shifted her gaze to the hand-crafted journals Vicki had organized for the bridal shower, fanned out next to the wine racks. An amazingly ornate quilt hung on a large frame and guests pointed and commented on it as they walked by.

"Isn't that gorgeous?" Bridgett asked. "The instant Vicki heard Miranda and Jesse were engaged, she asked everyone in town to donate a small swatch of fabric from their homes. Whether it was denim or satin, it didn't matter. She embroidered each contributor's name on their swatch with the new sewing machine Brandon bought her when Randi Lynn was born, and she made this community quilt for them."

"I can't even sew on a button," Tess said, "let alone churn that out in a few months. She's becoming quite the craftswoman."

"She should start her own business and you could

design her website," Bridgett said. "But not until you and Cole kiss and make up. Oh, look, here he is now."

Bridgett ran off before Tess could grab hold of her for protection. But it was only her heart that needed protecting. She wanted to tell Cole how much she loved him, had always loved him, but if she opened her mouth she knew tears would likely follow her confession and Miranda's wedding was not the time or the place. They'd already stolen the show at her shower.

Cole waved a small seating card in front of her with both of their names listed on it. Breaking yet another tradition, the bride and groom had their own quiet table for two at the head of the tent, while the wedding party and the guests flanked either side.

"It's good to see you." Cole's eyes immediately dropped to her bare left hand. Turning away, he offered her his arm and escorted to her to their seats.

Tess wanted to explain but before she had the chance, a waiter handed her a glass of champagne. Cole rose and tapped his glass with his knife.

"Growing up we all knew Jesse would be the first to get married. He was the calmest of the four of us and we assumed he would eventually find a nice girl to settle down with. Up until a few months ago, I believed that still held true until I was behind him on a trail and heard him saying 'I love you' over and over to the cattle. Turns out, he was practicing his proposal to Miranda, but for a moment, we were a little worried.

"Miranda, I've never seen my brother happier in his life. Marrying him means marrying into this crazy family of ours, and some would say we should be concerned about your sanity. But your spirit and determination not only won my brother's heart, they won the heart of an entire town.

"They say shared joy is a double joy and a shared sorrow is half a sorrow. I look around and see the happiness of this day shared among our closest friends, neighbors and family. May your troubles be few and far between, and lessened even more through the strength of your love together and the love of those surrounding you. Jesse and Miranda, congratulations. I love you both."

"That was beautiful," Tess said.

"It's no comparison to you."

COLE HAD WATCHED Tess from the moment she'd arrived at Double Trouble. He knew the bride was supposed to be the center of attention, but Tess's fitted, pale peach dress accentuated her slender curves and creamy skin, and the neckline dipped gracefully low, giving a hint of what lay underneath. The slit that fell midthigh stirred his arousal every time she crossed her legs.

Cole promised Jesse he'd oversee the reception area and insure their mother didn't exhaust herself before the ceremony. While the entire affair was catered, Kay wanted to add some of her own touches to the meal. Wine from the vineyard, fresh herbs from the garden and the honey-drizzled croissants she'd perfected with Maggie. She'd also created most of the table arrangements.

Miranda may have barreled into town with an attitude, but today she cemented her place in the family and their lives.

Tess's parents, Cole's mother and brothers rounded out their table. Shane and Chase both opted not to bring dates, with Shane hoping to find an out-of-town guest to sweep off her feet. One of these days he'd realize the one he should concentrate on stood straight across the tent from him, sneaking a peek whenever he wasn't looking. Cole saw his brother do the same thing with Lexi, and maybe someday she'd forgive him long enough to realize they were made for each other.

When the band began to play, Cole slid his chair out and offered Tess his hand. "May I have the honor?"

Tess coyly smiled, and, unlike senior prom, he wasn't afraid to hold her close. The smell of her perfume reminded him of coconut and gardenias. Her scents always bordered on the tropical and exotic, reconfirming she would have loved the Hawaiian destination wedding idea.

"I'm sorry—"

"I saw Ever—"

"Go ahead." Tess laughed.

"Did you say you saw Ever?"

"Yesterday, and it was the—"

"Medication that caused the seizure," Cole interrupted.

"You saw her, too?" Tess pulled back slightly, looking into his eyes.

"After Jesse's bachelor trip." Cole kept his arms wrapped around her, still swaying to the music. "The four of us went."

"You wouldn't be the mysterious teddy bear donor the nurse told me about when I called to check on Ever this morning?"

"I have no idea what you mean."

"Sure you don't." Tess looked up at him. "It was a terrific thing you did for those children. The hospital staff appreciates it and I'm sure they want to thank you."

"No one needs to know it was us." Pulling back, Cole looked into her eyes. "Sometimes giving anonymously is more rewarding than the world knowing what you've done."

Tess rested her head on his shoulder, and he relished the feel of her against him. She belonged with him, home in his arms.

"I've decided to go ahead with the adoption," Tess murmured against his chest. "I've already discussed it with Fannie and I hope you're still willing to be a part of it. I'm heading to the hospital to see Ever in the morning, if you'd care to join me."

"So that's what Fannie meant when she asked if I'd spoken with you." Cole stopped dancing and led her outside the tent and to the front porch. "I told Fannie I wanted to go ahead with the adoption, too."

They sat on the top step, overlooking the tents, guests milling about and children chasing one another. Jesse ran through the field, carrying Miranda in his arms, the sound of her laughter echoing throughout the ranch. This was the life he wanted. He'd never considered asking any other woman in his life to marry him. Tess hadn't said no, they hadn't broken off their engagement. She happened not to be wearing the ring today, but that was easily remedied.

"I have something to tell you, about Lorraine, but it can wait until after the wedding."

"Theirs?" Cole nodded toward the tents. "Or ours?

"You still want to marry me?" Tess asked.

"You're the one who took off the ring. I'm still status quo, sweetheart."

"I meant to put it back on this morning." Tess reached up and touched his face so he would look at her. "I shouldn't have taken it off."

"I love you, Tess," Cole shouted, jumping off the porch. "I've loved you since I first kissed you on your parents' porch swing, I loved you all throughout school,

I loved you in Vegas and I love you today and tomorrow and when we fly to Hawaii to get married."

"Shh, Cole." Tess giggled as she drew a finger to her lips, trying to silence him from the porch stairs. "I love you, too, but you're creating a scene."

"I promise to always be faithful to you," Cole announced loudly, sensing the crowd that had started to gather behind him. "And I swear to you, in front of the entire town, I've never given my heart to another woman."

"I believe you, Cole." Tess laughed. "You're insane, you know that? Wait, what did you say about flying to Hawaii to get married?"

"You were supposed to keep that a surprise!" Maggie shouted from the crowd.

"Fly away with me and make it official." Cole climbed the stairs, standing one step below her.

"My mother knows about Hawaii?" Tess looked over the top of his head.

"We all know" came a collective Langtry and Dalton shout.

"Do me the honor of being my wife." Cole took her hand in his. "And together we'll form our own family. For Ever."

Epilogue

Tess hastily signed for the package, unable to contain her excitement.

"What's that, Mommy?" Ever asked.

"Mommy and Daddy's wedding pictures." Tess removed the white satin photo album from the box and patted her lap. "Do you want to look through them with me?"

A month after Miranda and Jesse's wedding, Cole and Tess were married on Maui's Poolenalena Beach with hula skirts, leis and both of their families.

"Ricky wants to look, too." Ever patted her own lap, imitating Tess. The tabby crossed the newly renovated Hope's Cottage, which was given to them as a wedding gift from the Langtry family. The home's former beauty and simplicity had been restored and was idyllic for the three of them, thanks to all of Shane's hard work.

"This was Poolenalena Beach." Tess pointed to the photo of both families, the setting sun in the background. "Can you say Poo-len-a-lena?"

"Poo..." Ever giggled.

"I'll poo you." Tess tickled her daughter. "Look how handsome Daddy was."

"Where are his shoes?" Ever pointed to the photo of a barefoot Cole in a white linen suit.

"You don't wear shoes on the beach," Tess said. "Daddy and I will take you someday."

"I wish I was there," Ever said. "But I wasn't yours yet."

"I wish you had been there, too." Tess kissed the top of her daughter's head while they turned the pages.

Ever had come to live with them shortly after they returned home. Tess and Cole invited Lorraine to remain an active part of Ever's life, feeling their daughter could never be surrounded by too much love.

"Where's my angel?" Cole called from the front door.

Sliding off Tess's lap, Ever walked over to Cole with only the aid of her braces. The sight of them together still warmed Tess's heart every time.

"Daddy, the wedding pictures came."

"Hello, beautiful." Cole lightly kissed Tess and joined them on the couch. Whenever the big-city bug nipped at Tess, all she had to do was take one look at her daughter and her husband and think of their happiness on the ranch. "It's amazing how much has changed since then."

"The babies are coming soon," Ever sang. "I'm going to have cousins."

"Miranda has a few more months to go, sweetie," Tess said as she laughed.

On Christmas day, Miranda and Jesse had received a surprise of their own when a pregnancy test turned out positive. The twins were expected in August and all Ever could talk about was how she'd teach them to ride horses.

"After dinner we'll ride down and see the arena." Cole beamed when talking about the new state-of-the-art equine facility. "They set the roof today and you can really see it coming together."

"When are you boys going to tell Kay you're naming her CEO of Dance of Hope?"

"Chase thought maybe for her birthday in June, but I wanted to run it by everyone first. I almost hate to wait that long."

"Now I know where Ever gets her impatience from," Tess teased. "It's a Langtry thing."

"Hey, now." Cole grabbed Ever by the waist and lifted her in the air. "We're not impatient, are we, princess? But Poncho might be if we don't go feed him."

"Okay." Ever squealed and giggled. Cole had traded another horse in exchange for Poncho so Ever's beloved horse would always be near.

"You don't even know what *impatient* means, silly girl." Tess loved the way the sound of their daughter's sweet laughter filled the ranch. Ever and Tess had both come home to their cowboy.

"At least both my girls are happy," Cole said. "What more could a man ask for?"

* * * * *

COMING NEXT MONTH
from Harlequin® American Romance®

AVAILABLE SEPTEMBER 3, 2013

#1465 CALLAHAN COWBOY TRIPLETS
Callahan Cowboys
Tina Leonard

For Tighe Callahan, the upside of being injured in a bull-riding accident is sexy River Martin appointing herself his nurse. Now if only she'll let him take care of her...and their three babies on the way!

#1466 A NAVY SEAL'S SURPRISE BABY
Operation: Family
Laura Marie Altom

Navy SEAL Calder Remington is shocked when he finds out he's a daddy. But he's even more surprised when he begins to have real feelings for Pandora Moore—his son's nanny!

#1467 HOME TO WYOMING
Daddy Dude Ranch
Rebecca Winters

Buck Summerhayes never thought he would meet the right woman, but from the moment he sees Alexis Wilson, Buck knows she's for him. Too bad she's completely off-limits....

#1468 HAVING THE COWBOY'S BABY
Blue Falls, Texas
Trish Milburn

The last thing organized, uptight Skyler Harrington needs is an unplanned pregnancy, but that's what she gets after letting go for one night and sleeping with sexy cowboy Logan Bradshaw.

You can find more information on upcoming Harlequin® titles, free excerpts and more at www.Harlequin.com.

REQUEST YOUR FREE BOOKS!
2 FREE NOVELS PLUS 2 FREE GIFTS!

♦ HARLEQUIN®

American ★ Romance®

LOVE, HOME & HAPPINESS

YES! Please send me 2 FREE Harlequin® American Romance® novels and my 2 FREE gifts (gifts are worth about $10). After receiving them, if I don't wish to receive any more books, I can return the shipping statement marked "cancel." If I don't cancel, I will receive 4 brand-new novels every month and be billed just $4.74 per book in the U.S. or $5.24 per book in Canada. That's a savings of at least 14% off the cover price! It's quite a bargain! Shipping and handling is just 50¢ per book in the U.S. and 75¢ per book in Canada.* I understand that accepting the 2 free books and gifts places me under no obligation to buy anything. I can always return a shipment and cancel at any time. Even if I never buy another book, the two free books and gifts are mine to keep forever.

154/354 HDN F4YN

Name _____ (PLEASE PRINT)

Address _____ Apt. #

City _____ State/Prov. _____ Zip/Postal Code

Signature (if under 18, a parent or guardian must sign)

Mail to the **Harlequin® Reader Service:**
IN U.S.A.: P.O. Box 1867, Buffalo, NY 14240-1867
IN CANADA: P.O. Box 609, Fort Erie, Ontario L2A 5X3

Want to try two free books from another line?
Call 1-800-873-8635 or visit www.ReaderService.com.

* Terms and prices subject to change without notice. Prices do not include applicable taxes. Sales tax applicable in N.Y. Canadian residents will be charged applicable taxes. Offer not valid in Quebec. This offer is limited to one order per household. Not valid for current subscribers to Harlequin American Romance books. All orders subject to credit approval. Credit or debit balances in a customer's account(s) may be offset by any other outstanding balance owed by or to the customer. Please allow 4 to 6 weeks for delivery. Offer available while quantities last.

Your Privacy—The Harlequin® Reader Service is committed to protecting your privacy. Our Privacy Policy is available online at www.ReaderService.com or upon request from the Harlequin Reader Service.

We make a portion of our mailing list available to reputable third parties that offer products we believe may interest you. If you prefer that we not exchange your name with third parties, or if you wish to clarify or modify your communication preferences, please visit us at www.ReaderService.com/consumerschoice or write to us at Harlequin Reader Service Preference Service, P.O. Box 9062, Buffalo, NY 14269. Include your complete name and address.

HAR13R

SPECIAL EXCERPT FROM

H HARLEQUIN®

TM

American Romance®

Check out this excerpt from
CALLAHAN COWBOY TRIPLETS
by Tina Leonard,
coming September 2013.

Tighe, the wildest of the Callahan brothers, is determined
to have his eight seconds of glory in the bull-riding ring—
but gorgeous River Martin throws off his game!

Tighe Callahan sized up the enormous spotted bull. "Hello, Firefreak," he said. "You may have bested my twin, Dante, but I aim to ride you until you're soft as glove leather. Gonna retire you to the kiddie rides."

The legendary rank bull snorted a heavy breath his way, daring him.

"You're crazy, Tighe," his brother Jace said. "I'm telling you, that one wants to kill you."

"Feeling's mutual." Tighe grinned and knocked on the wall of the pen that held the bull. "If Dante stayed on him for five seconds, I ought to at least go ten."

Jace looked at Tighe doubtfully. "Sure. You can do it. Whatever." He glanced around. "I think I'll go get some popcorn and find a pretty girl to share it with. You and Firefreak just go ahead and chat about life. May be a one-sided conversation, but those are your favorite, anyway."

Jace wandered off. Tighe studied the bull, who never broke eye contact with him, his gaze wise with the scores of cowboys whom he'd mercilessly tossed, earning himself a legendary status.

"Hi, Tighe," River Martin said, and Tighe felt his heart start to palpitate. Here was his dream, his unattainable brunette princess—smiling at him as sweet as cherry wine. "We heard you're going to ride a bull tomorrow, so the girls and I decided to come out and watch."

This wasn't good. A man didn't need his concentration wrecked by a gorgeous female—nor did he want said gorgeous, unattainable female to see him get squashed by a few tons of angry luggage with horns.

But River was smiling at him with her teasing eyes, so all Tighe could say was, "Nice of you ladies to come out."

River said, "Good luck," and Tighe shivered, because he did believe in magic and luck and everything spiritual. And any superstitious man knew it was taunting the devil himself to wish a man good luck when the challenge he faced in the ring was nothing compared to the real challenge: forcing himself to look into a woman's sexy gaze and not drown.

He was drowning, and he had been for oh, so long.

Look for CALLAHAN COWBOY TRIPLETS by Tina Leonard, coming September 2013, only from Harlequin® American Romance®.

Copyright © 2013 by Tina Leonard

SADDLE UP AND READ 'EM!

Looking for another great Western read? Check out these September reads from HOME & FAMILY category!

CALLAHAN COWBOY TRIPLETS by Tina Leonard
Callahan Cowboys
Harlequin American Romance

HAVING THE COWBOY'S BABY by Trish Milburn
Blue Falls, Texas
Harlequin American Romance

HOME TO WYOMING by Rebecca Winters
Daddy Dude Ranch
Harlequin American Romance

*Look for these great Western reads and more
available wherever books are sold or visit*
www.Harlequin.com/Westerns

SUART0913HF

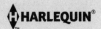

American Romance®

Wounded in love and war.

Ex-marine Buck Summerhayes wants to put the past behind him. He finds peace working at the Teton Valley Dude Ranch, a special place for families of fallen soldiers. Maybe one day, he'll have a family of his own—right now, he can't afford to indulge in dreams.

Alexis Wilson is no dream. Tasked with overseeing Alex and her young ward during their visit to the ranch, Buck finds himself falling for both the woman and the little girl. Like Buck, Alex has had more than her share of heartache. But maybe between them, they can build a future that's still full of possibilities.

Home to Wyoming

by REBECCA WINTERS

Dare to dream on September 3, only from
Harlequin® American Romance®.

www.Harlequin.com

HAR75471

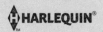
HARLEQUIN®

American Romance®

There's just something about a cowboy....

Skyler Harrington is a planner. After the tumult of her childhood, she's built a life for herself in Blue Falls, Texas, that's comfortable, predictable, safe. The last thing she needs is to go gaga over a rodeo cowboy. It felt great to let her hair down with sexy Logan Bradshaw, but she'll be happy if their paths never cross again.

A surprise pregnancy is something neither expected. She's willing to raise their child alone, but Logan is determined to prove he's more than a devil-may-care risk taker. He's daddy material!

Don't miss

Having the Cowboy's Baby

by TRISH MILBURN

**Available September 3, only from
Harlequin® American Romance®.**

www.Harlequin.com

HAR75472